Best Kept Secret

ALSO BY ANN M. MARTIN:

Belle Teal

A Corner of the Universe

A Dog's Life

Everything for a Dog

Here Today

On Christmas Eve

P.S. Longer Letter Later
written with Paula Danziger

Snail Mail No More
written with Paula Danziger

Ten Good and Bad Things About My Life (So Far)

Ten Kids, No Pets

Ten Rules for Living with My Sister

The Baby-sitters Club series

The Doll People series
written with Laura Godwin

The Main Street series

Family Tree

Best Kept Secret

The Third Generation

ANN M. MARTIN

Scholastic Press / New York

For Jane, Doug, and Henry,
with love and laughter

Copyright © 2014 by Ann M. Martin

All rights reserved. Published by Scholastic Press, an imprint of Scholastic Inc.,
Publishers since 1920. SCHOLASTIC, SCHOLASTIC PRESS, and associated logos are trademarks
and/or registered trademarks of Scholastic Inc.

Library of Congress Cataloging-in-Publication Data

Martin, Ann M., 1955– author.
Best kept secret : the third generation / Ann M. Martin. — First edition.
pages cm. — (Family tree ; book 3)
Summary: In 1977 in Princeton, Dana's daughter, seven-year-old Francie, is struggling to
keep her dyslexia a secret from her teachers and family, and even the thought of high
school and college is part of the remote and unattainable future.
ISBN 978-0-545-35944-3 (jacketed hardcover) 1. Dyslexia — Juvenile fiction.
2. Schools — Juvenile fiction. 3. Families — New Jersey — Princeton — Juvenile fiction.
4. Mothers and daughters — Juvenile fiction. 5. Princeton (N.J.) — History — 20th
century — Juvenile fiction. [1. Dyslexia — Fiction. 2. Schools — Fiction. 3. Family
life — New Jersey — Princeton — Fiction. 4. Mothers and daughters — Fiction.
5. Princeton (N.J.) — History — 20th century — Fiction.] I. Title. II. Series: Martin,
Ann M., 1955- Family tree ; bk. 3.
PZ7.M3567585Bek 2014
813.54 — dc23
2013032027

10 9 8 7 6 5 4 3 2 1   14 15 16 17 18

Printed in the U.S.A.   23
First edition, May 2014

The text type was set in Baskerville MT.
Book design by Elizabeth B. Parisi

Chapter 1

Thursday, July 14th, 1977

The first thing Francie Goldberg's eyes focused on as she struggled awake that morning was a copy of *Hop on Pop*. It was sitting on the little desk that her father had refinished and painted for her the previous summer. He had worked on the desk for many evenings — many evenings that Francie had spent sitting cross-legged on the floor of his studio upstairs, watching as he magically coaxed fairies and twining vines out of the white paint.

"Every first grader needs a desk," he had said to her as he'd poised his brush above a knob on one of the drawers.

"Why?" Francie had asked.

"Because you're going to have homework. You'll need a place for your workbooks and pencils."

Homework. The very word had made Francie feel proud. She was going to learn to read in first grade, and she would have homework like her friend Amy Fox, who lived next door and was a year older and came home from school every day with important-looking papers sticking out of a green folder.

But now a whole year had gone by — all of first grade — and while Francie had indeed been sent home with homework, she'd spent a year struggling through exercises and trying to keep up with the students in the Red Wagon Group, which every kid in her class knew was the lowest of the three reading groups, no matter what it was called. Francie couldn't even keep up with the slow readers. She could barely read at all. Letters flipped themselves around and upside down. A *p* looked just like a *d* or a *b*, and words seemed to shift on her. Really, what was the difference between *read* and *dear* or *pets* and *pest* or, for that matter, between *kitchen* and *chicken*?

This was why three times a week, all summer long, she had to endure a visit from Mrs. Travers, with her work sheets and flash cards and suggestions to her parents that they buy Francie *Hop on Pop* and *One Fish Two Fish Red Fish Blue Fish*.

From across her bedroom, Francie stuck out her tongue at *Hop on Pop*. She hated that book. She'd gone to all the trouble of memorizing it so that she could tell Mrs. Travers she could read after all, and then Mrs. Travers had opened to a page in the middle and told Francie to read it and Francie hadn't known where to begin without beginning at the beginning.

At least Mrs. Travers wouldn't be coming today. Thursday was not a Mrs. Travers day.

Francie sat up in bed and peered through her open window. She listened to the sound of traffic on Nassau Street — Princeton, New Jersey's, main street — which was a block away. The air drifting into her room was already hot. It smelled like grass and sunshine and the lavender plants that lined the walkway to the front door of her house. She looked at her yard below, with the flower gardens that her mother tended, and then across the street to the Newcomers' large Victorian house, with its many bedrooms and five Newcomer children. Francie's house was equally large, but the only people living in it were her and her parents, Dana and Matthew.

Francie padded into the hallway. She was about to make her way downstairs when she noticed that the door to the room next to hers was closed. This was one of the guest rooms, and the door had been open when Francie had gone to bed the night before. She quickened her pace and ran to the kitchen.

"Hi, Dana!" she said to her mother. (Francie's parents, unlike the parents of most of her friends, preferred to be called by their first names.)

"Morning, pumpkin."

Francie slid into her place at the table. "Why is the guest room door closed?" she asked.

Dana, who was busy at the coffeemaker, turned around and smiled. "Guess who's here," she said.

Francie thought for a moment. "Grandpa Arnold and Nonnie?" she asked, even though her father's parents lived only an hour away and rarely stayed overnight with the Goldbergs.

Dana shook her head.

"Adele?" said Francie, excitement blooming. "Is Adele here?"

"Yes, I am," said her great-aunt from the doorway.

Francie jumped up from her chair and ran to Adele. "You *are* here!" She paused. "But *why*? I didn't know you were coming."

Adele laughed and then stifled a yawn. "I didn't know I was coming either. But when I was driving back home last night after a little vacation, I heard on the news that there was a blackout in New York. Most of the city is without power, so I decided to come here instead of going to my apartment."

"A blackout," Francie repeated. "Ooh. Scary." The few times the power had gone out in Princeton, the Goldbergs had pretended they were pioneers and had eaten meals by candlelight and told one another stories, since they couldn't watch TV. That had been fun. But Francie wasn't sure she'd want to be in a city the size of New York without electricity.

"It *is* scary," agreed Adele. "Think of all the things in a city that don't work without power. Elevators — not that there's an elevator in my building, but still. Streetlights, traffic lights. And I don't even want to think about the subways. So I'm going to stay here until the power's back."

"I hope that's not for a long time," said Francie. "A long, long time." Adele, who was Dana's aunt, was Francie's favorite person in the whole world except for her parents and Amy Fox. "Is Bobbie Palombo's closed?"

"I suppose so," replied Adele. "I think everything is closed." Adele worked for a woman named Bobbie Palombo, designing costumes for Broadway shows. Because of this, she went to the theatre all the time and had already taken Francie to see *Hello, Dolly!* and *Gypsy*. Francie thought that, maybe, when she grew up, she might design costumes, too. *Maybe*. She wasn't sure. It was hard to think that far ahead.

Adele took a seat at the table and Dana handed her a cup of coffee. Adele yawned again. "Where's Matthew?" she asked.

"Upstairs. He's just waking up," replied Francie's mother. "He worked until after two last night. He's going to have to get a move on, though. He's helping with a new exhibit at the art museum. He's supposed to be over there in an hour."

"And you?" Adele asked. "What are you doing today?"

5

"Putting the finishing touches on *Grizzly Bob*. It's due in two weeks."

Francie put her chin in her hand and stared out the kitchen window at the backyard. Her parents were hard to keep up with. They were the busiest people she knew, especially when you considered that neither of them had a regular job like her friends' parents had. Amy's father took the train into New York City five mornings a week and worked at an investment firm (whatever that was). Mr. Newcomer left his house every day at eight o'clock to work at a Princeton company called ETS, which had something to do with tests, while Mrs. Newcomer worked three afternoons a week in a store on Nassau Street. Those were regular jobs.

Francie's parents were artists. Her father did have an office at Princeton University, because during the school year, he taught art courses there. Otherwise he worked in his third-floor studio at home, creating paintings that people all over the world wanted to buy. He worked whenever he felt like it, even if it was late at night or on a weekend. The room next to his studio was Dana's studio. Dana illustrated children's picture books. Sometimes she illustrated *and* wrote them. The books were very popular and it seemed to Francie that her mother was always running off to sign books for long lines of people who came to stores just to see her, or flying to conferences to talk about her work. Once she won an award for one of her books, and Francie and Matthew flew with her to San Francisco for a big ceremony.

Francie couldn't have felt more different from her parents. She excelled at nothing. She couldn't even read the books her mother had written, let alone all the fat books lining the walls of their den. She had no interest in painting or in drawing. There was a piano in their living room, but Francie never sat at it. What she liked to do, mostly, was make up stories in her head. But sometimes she found it hard to entertain herself on long summer days.

"Well," Adele said to Francie now, "if your mom is working on *Grizzly Bob* and your dad is due on campus, then I guess it's just you and me today. What do you want to do?"

"Can we ride around in your car?" Francie asked. Adele drove an old blue Renault with a convertible top. She kept plaid bandanas in the glove compartment, and Francie always tied one under her chin when the top was down.

"Absolutely," Adele replied.

"Can we get pizza from Conte's for lunch?"

"Absolutely."

(Adele almost never said no.)

Half an hour later, Matthew left for the art museum on the university campus and Dana disappeared upstairs to her studio. Francie and Adele tied on their bandanas and took a drive through Princeton. They rode along beside Carnegie Lake, where Francie and Amy went ice-skating in the winter. They made a big circle back through town, passed by the library and the YWCA, kept on going, and finally stopped at the playground in Marquand Park, before picking up pizza slices at Conte's. As they drove down Vandeventer Avenue, Francie waved proudly to Amy and three of the Newcomer kids, who were playing freeze tag in Amy's yard.

"Could we have a pizza picnic?" Francie asked as Adele parked the convertible in the Goldbergs' driveway.

"Absolutely."

Francie and Adele ate their pizza, sitting on a bedspread in the shade of an elm tree in the backyard.

"Now what?" Francie asked when her last slice was gone.

"Getting bored?"

"I'm just not sure what we should do next."

"How about walking to the campus and visiting your father?"

"Yes!" exclaimed Francie, jumping to her feet.

She took Adele's hand and they walked down Vandeventer in the direction of Nassau Street. They crossed Nassau and entered the world of Princeton University. It was only yards from the shops and businesses on Nassau, but it felt like a different world — looming brick and stone buildings from other centuries, tree-lined walkways between dormitories and classrooms. The university had its own chapel and its own art museum and its own stadium. The oldest Newcomer kid claimed that one day she was going to go to Princeton University. Francie was in awe of this ambition, considering that she herself couldn't even read.

Francie and Adele stepped inside the museum and the first person they saw was a graduate student named Stella, who was Matthew's assistant that summer. She was walking into one of the galleries with a wrapped painting under her arm.

"Hi, Francie!" called Stella. "What are you doing here?"

"Looking for Matthew. This is my aunt Adele."

Adele and Stella shook hands, and Stella said that Matthew had gone to his office for a while, so off went Francie and Adele through the campus again. They found Matthew sitting behind his big cluttered desk, his feet on a pile of books.

Francie giggled. "I think he's sleeping," she whispered to Adele.

Matthew opened one eye and smiled. "No, I'm not. I'm planning a painting in my head." This was what Francie's father always said when he was caught with his eyes closed.

"We just stopped by to say hello," said Adele.

"Are you coming home soon?" asked Francie.

9

"In time for dinner. I'm due back at the museum in a few minutes. What have you been up to?"

Francie told her father about their adventures. Then she and Adele walked Matthew back to the museum, Francie jumping in and out of the stone gutters that lined the pathways through campus.

At the Goldbergs' house, Adele phoned Bobbie Palombo and then reported to Dana, who was still working, that the power was coming back on in New York, neighborhood by neighborhood. "I'd better be on my way," she said.

"No!" wailed Francie. "Please stay until tomorrow."

Adele gave her a hug. "Can't. I have to get back to work. I've already been away for several days. But this was a nice, unexpected end to my vacation."

Half an hour later, Francie watched Adele pull the Renault onto Vandeventer and into the traffic on Nassau. Once Adele was gone, Francie ran next door to Amy's and rang her bell. No answer. Francie wasn't allowed to cross Vandeventer without an adult yet, so she couldn't go to the Newcomers' house. Instead, she continued past Amy's to the Horans'. Mrs. Horan told her the twins had gone to the community swimming pool with Amy, which figured, because the twins were Amy's age and always asked Amy to do things with them before they thought of asking Francie. Francie rang the Friedmans' door,

x

10

but found only Jeanie Friedman's grandfather there. Mr. Friedman was very nice, and, the year before, had given Francie a silver charm for her bracelet on the eighth night of Hanukkah. But Francie was looking for someone her own age.

She scuffed her feet as she returned slowly to her house. She wished Amy were at home. She wished she had a very best friend who was almost seven like her and going into second grade at school. She wished she could read. She wished she had a dog.

She was climbing the steps to her front porch, eyes downcast, her thoughts on a dog, when she was startled to hear her mother say, "Hi, pumpkin."

There was Dana, sitting in a rocker, a glass of iced tea beside her.

"Hi!" cried Francie.

"I'm done with *Grizzly Bob* for the day," said her mother. "Would you like to go to the pool in a little while?"

"Absolutely."

Francie flew up the stairs to her room and changed into her bathing suit. Later, as she rode along Witherspoon Street with Dana, the loneliness of the last hour vanished and a summer evening with her parents stretched ahead. She suddenly realized that she might not understand her mother, but that her mother would always be there for her, steady and sure.

Chapter 2

"Guess what today is," Francie said as she and Dana and Matthew hurried through their breakfast. "It's my seventh day of being seven years old."

Her parents laughed.

"Not to mention your first day of second grade," said Dana.

Francie put her spoon down and screwed up her face.

"Nervous?" asked Matthew.

"A little."

"But you've already met Mr. Ellis and you liked him," Dana reminded her.

"I know." Mr. Ellis was fine. Francie wasn't nervous about her teacher. But she was afraid that the last day of second grade would roll around and she still wouldn't know how to read. She was going to have special reading help this year and she'd continue working with Mrs. Travers after school, but what if she *never* learned to read?

"I have a funny feeling that you're worrying about something in the future," said Dana. "Are you? Are you thinking about something beyond today?"

Francie nodded.

"Do you want to talk about it?"

Francie shook her head.

"Well then, one step at a time," said Matthew. "First, let's get you to school."

"Are you sure you both need to walk with me?" asked Francie, who was aware that Amy and the twins were going to walk to school by themselves. They would probably pass Francie walking with Dana and Matthew, but Francie hadn't been able to talk her parents out of this.

"We just want to say hi to Mr. Ellis," said Matthew.

"And I have a feeling we won't be the only parents walking their kids to school today," added Dana.

Dana was right. Francie saw plenty of parents that morning. She saw the Newcomers walking hand in hand down their driveway with their youngest child (a kindergartener). And she saw Mr. and Mrs. Friedman, plus old Mr. Friedman, taking Jeanie to school.

"Well, here we are," said Matthew, at last, as they stood outside Mr. Ellis's room. "Are you ready for second grade?"

Francie looked at the large sunflower that Mr. Ellis had taped to the door. She looked inside at Mr. Ellis's smiling face. "I hope so," she said.

To Francie's relief, her parents stayed barely long enough to shake Mr. Ellis's hand. They greeted several other parents, and then all the parents left in a great bunch.

Mr. Ellis looked at the twenty students sitting at the twenty desks in his room. He closed the door and said, "Welcome to second grade. I'm Mr. Ellis. The very first thing we're going to do today is get to know one another. Please introduce yourselves to your neighbors."

Francie turned to the girl on her right. The girl looked familiar, but Francie didn't know her name. "Hi. I'm Francie," she said.

"I'm Kaycee Noble," the girl replied. Her thick dark hair was pulled into a messy ponytail, and she was wearing a T-shirt with a lobster on the front. "Only you spell it *K-A-Y-C-E-E*," she went on, "not *C-A-S-E-Y*. Because it's for my initials, *K* and *C*. Katherine Christine. Get it?"

Francie only sort of got it, since this seemed a lot like reading. So instead, she answered, "I like your T-shirt."

"We went to Maine this summer."

"Really? My cousins live in Maine!" exclaimed Francie. "My aunts and uncles, too. We go there every summer. And sometimes in between." She turned to the boy on her left, who hadn't been in her first-grade class either. "Hi. I'm Francie," she said.

"Good for you" was his rude reply.

Francie rolled her eyes and turned back to Kaycee.

The morning continued. Mr. Ellis took attendance. He told the students what he expected of them as second graders. He moved several of the students, including the rude boy, to different desks, but left Francie and Kaycee next to each other in the third row. He invited the students to share their summer experiences, and Francie felt pleased when both she and Kaycee talked about their trips to Maine.

At ten thirty, the door to the room opened and a woman Francie recognized as the Resource Room teacher pointed to her and nodded. The rude boy snickered as Francie left her seat, but Kaycee just looked on curiously, offering Francie a smile. Francie spent the next hour working side by side with Mrs. Pownell, once again thrust into the mysterious world of letters and sounds.

"We'll be working together for an hour every morning and an hour every afternoon," Mrs. Pownell told Francie. "Just on reading. You're so smart in math and science that I want you in Mr. Ellis's room for those subjects."

Smart? Francie hadn't heard her first-grade teacher say she was smart. And certainly Mrs. Travers had never called her smart. Francie walked jubilantly back to her classroom just as Mr. Ellis said, "Class, please open your math books."

When math ended, it was finally time for lunch and recess.

"Sit with me," said Kaycee as Francie and their classmates, following Mr. Ellis two by two, made their way to the lunchroom.

Francie saw some of her friends from first grade, but decided to sit at the end of a table across from Kaycee, several places away from three of the boys in their class, including the one who had laughed when Francie had left for the Resource Room.

"Don't pay any attention to him," whispered Kaycee, jerking her head toward the boy.

"How did you know I was thinking about him?" asked Francie.

"I could just tell. Anyway, he's mean and the best thing is to ignore him."

"But he laughed at me."

"So what? He's a bully. The rest of them are, too. And Mr. Ellis knows it. That's why he switched them around. He doesn't want them sitting next to each other. I don't even remember their names," Kaycee went on (rather loudly,

Francie thought), "and I'll bet you don't either. Their names aren't worth remembering."

Francie giggled.

"Our names are Jake and Jed and Antoine!" one of the boys called. "I'm Jake, he's Jed, and he's Antoine."

"Good for you," said Francie.

She and Kaycee ignored the boys and talked about Maine some more. When, at last, they finished their lunches, they tossed the crumpled paper bags in the trash. Kaycee took Francie's hand and they ran to the playground.

"The swings are free," announced Kaycee. "Come on!"

"But you're wearing a dress." Francie, who was wearing blue jeans, was horrified. There were certain pieces of playground equipment to be avoided if you were wearing a dress, and everyone knew it.

Kaycee shrugged and said, "So what?"

So Francie shrugged, too. "Okay!"

She and Kaycee claimed adjacent swings and began to pump. Francie gripped the chain of the swing with her left hand and Kaycee's hand with her right.

"Did you know," said Kaycee as they rose higher and higher, "that if you pump hard enough, you can go all the way over the top of the swing and make a full circle? That means you're upside down —"

Francie, eyes wide, was listening breathlessly to Kaycee, when from below she heard the sound of several voices chanting, "I see London, I see France! I see Kaycee's underpants!" As the swings arced backward, Francie caught sight of the smug faces of Jake, Jed, and Antoine, and her cheeks began to flame. She was horribly embarrassed for her new friend.

The boys whispered to one another for a moment and then, as Francie and Kaycee once more whizzed past them, Francie heard something new.

"I see London, I see Francie! She's not wearing underpantsies!"

"Hey!" she cried. "I am, too, wearing underpants. You just can't see them."

"Prove it," said the rude boy.

Kaycee let go of Francie's hand and dragged her swing to a stop. Francie slowed down beside her.

"Which one are you?" asked Kaycee, pointing to the boy.

"Antoine," he replied.

"No, he's not," Francie said triumphantly. "He's Jed. I remember."

"If you're so smart, how come you have to go to the Resource Room?" asked Jed.

"If *you're* so smart, how come your shirt's on backward?"

Kaycee eyed Jed pityingly. When he glanced down, she cried, "Ha! Made you look!"

Antoine and Jake laughed uncertainly at that. But Jed wasn't about to give up. "Come on," he said to Francie. "Show us your underwear."

"No."

The boys began a new chant. "Francie, Francie, Francie! Not wearing underpantsies! Francie, Francie, Francie! Not wearing underpantsies!"

Francie took a step back and raised her fist.

"Wait!" said Kaycee, catching Francie's arm. "Don't. That's just what they want. Come on. Let's go play princess." She turned to the boys. "And don't follow us. Because in our kingdom, the princesses are *in charge*."

The boys backed away, muttering things about underwear, and Francie allowed Kaycee to lead her across the playground.

It felt good to be a princess in charge.

That afternoon, Mrs. Pownell once again arrived at the door of Mr. Ellis's room and nodded to Francie. Francie glanced at Jed and saw that he had opened his mouth, probably to say something about the Resource Room, but he closed it abruptly when he saw Kaycee glaring at him from her seat. Francie grinned and followed Mrs. Pownell down the hall.

When school ended, Francie said good-bye to Kaycee and waited by the front door of the school for Amy. After a few minutes, Amy sauntered out, followed by Connie and Polly Horan, all carrying very full book bags.

"Guess what our homework is tonight," said Amy. "We have to cover our books."

"We have a reader and a math book and a social studies book," added Connie.

"And we have to make covers for them out of paper bags," said Polly.

"Oh," said Francie, who had a pile of workbooks, but nothing that required covering. Still, she now had a folder for her special homework from Mrs. Pownell, homework she was certain she could complete all by herself.

The girls walked to Vandeventer. When Francie reached her house, she peeked into the third-floor studios and found both her parents absorbed in their artwork. She wondered how grown-ups could concentrate like that.

By dinnertime, her homework was finished. Francie proudly showed it to Matthew and Dana.

"That's wonderful," said her father as he set a bowl of pasta on the table.

Dana looked thoughtful. "We've been talking about something," she said.

Uh-oh. Alarm bells rang in Francie's head. "What?" she asked.

"We were thinking that, this year, you should take lessons of some kind."

"Or join a team," added Matthew.

"Give ballet a try. Or piano. Or soccer. *Something.*"

Francie sighed. "Maybe." She fiddled with her napkin. "Can I go over to Amy's after dinner? It's still light out."

Dana heaved a sigh of her own. "Sure."

Later, Francie escaped across her lawn, ran to the Foxes' house, and rang the bell. She was greeted by the barking of Amy's dog, Hank.

"Hank, Hank! It's me!" Francie called.

The barking stopped and Amy opened the door. "Guess what!" she exclaimed.

"What?"

"Come in and I'll show you."

Amy, followed by her little brother, Max, led Francie into the living room. Leaning against an armchair was what looked like an enormous violin.

"Ta-da!" said Amy. "That's my dad's cello. I'm going to start taking lessons."

"Wow," said Francie in a small voice. Then she added, "I might take lessons, too."

"What kind of lessons?"

Francie shrugged. She had no idea.

But she didn't want to be left out again.

Chapter 3

Francie sat at her desk, paging through her reader. It wasn't the same reader Kaycee had been given on the first day of third grade. But still, it was a reader, an actual reader. More important, Francie could read the words in it all by herself. Most of them anyway. And when she didn't immediately recognize a word, she knew ways to figure it out. She could read the rest of the sentence for clues, or she could think about her letter rules, such as what a tricky silent *E* at the end of a word could do to a vowel in the middle.

"Francie," Mrs. Pownell had said on the last day of second grade, sounding very serious, "we're not going to be seeing each other next year."

Francie's breath had caught in her chest. She loved Mrs. Pownell. "Are you moving away?" she'd whispered.

Mrs. Pownell had smiled at her. "No. I'll still be here. But you won't be my student. You don't need the Resource Room anymore. You've outgrown it."

Francie hadn't known whether to be pleased or terrified. "Are you sure?" she'd said finally.

"Quite sure. You've made great strides. As long as you work with Mrs. Travers at home a couple of times a week, you'll be fine."

"But . . . but . . ."

"I'll always be here if you need me," Mrs. Pownell had gone on. "But I don't think you will. Come by and say hello, though, anytime you want to visit. I'll miss you."

Francie, who had taken several tests with Mrs. Pownell during second grade, knew now that she had a reading condition called dyslexia.

"See? I'm not stupid," she had said triumphantly to her parents on the day Mrs. Pownell had discussed the test results with the Goldbergs.

Her parents had looked shocked. "Francie!" Dana had exclaimed. "We *never* thought you were stupid."

"No, but Jake and Jed and a lot of kids in my class think I am."

"The truth is," Mrs. Pownell had said seriously, "you're probably one of the smartest kids in your entire grade — but you have to work twice as hard as anyone else because of your dyslexia. It's hard for you to process what you read and to remember the sequence of things you read. It's even hard for you to control your eye movements across the page as you read. You *can* do all those things, but it takes extra concentration."

Francie had sighed. "Will it always be like this?"

"Will it always be so hard? Maybe, but probably not. I think it will get easier as you get older. You're going to have to remember your tricks, though. Read slowly. Make sure that what you're reading makes sense. Use your Magic Window card to see one word at a time if you're getting confused —"

"And my ruler to focus on one line at a time," added Francie.

"Exactly. And you'll always have to remember to —"

"Check my work!" Francie finished for her. "I know, I know. Check it once, then check it again."

Mrs. Pownell had smiled. "It will be worth it."

Now third grade had begun, and while Francie worked with Mrs. Travers every Tuesday and Thursday after school, she no longer went to the Resource Room. She held her head high in Ms. Annich's class. More important, she had finally found a talent. A real talent.

Francie Goldberg was a storyteller.

She could make up the best stories of anyone in her class. Writing them down wasn't always easy, because in addition to struggling with her reading, she was a horrible speller. Which made sense, if you thought about it. Francie had neat, precise handwriting — but her spelling was atrocious. So sometimes when she had a particularly good story that she needed to get down on paper, she would dictate it to Dana or Matthew.

"And to think that you discovered your storytelling talent because of the piano," Matthew would say to Francie with a smile.

This was a family joke. After Amy Fox had decided to take up the cello, Francie had consented to start piano lessons, if for no other reason than because the Goldbergs already had a piano. But she had hated the lessons, she had hated practicing, and she had hated her piano books.

"See?" she'd said to her father one rainy day, several months after the loathsome lessons had begun. She'd waved one of her piano books in his face.

"See what?" Matthew had asked. He'd set down his paintbrush and given her his full attention.

"See how stupid these lessons are? Listen to this song I'm supposed to learn to play." She'd opened the book. "These are really the words: 'Porcupines have prickly quills. Don't go near their favorite hills. If you do, you'll have bad luck, 'cause you surely will get stuck.'" Francie had rolled her eyes. "That is so lame. What's a porcupine hill anyway? Porcupines live in trees or dens. Whoever wrote that song just used *hills* because it rhymes with *quills*. That is not good writing. It's *lazy*."

"Well, you don't have to *sing* the song," Matthew had said. "You just have to play the tune."

"I know but . . . I could write better than that."

"So write better than that."

A week later, the piano lessons had come to an end.

"Francie!" Dana called now from downstairs. "Get a move on!"

"I want to finish my homework first. I'm almost done."

"I'm glad you're eager to finish your homework, but come on! We're supposed to meet Kaycee and her family in fifteen minutes."

Francie closed the reader, which she had meticulously covered with a paper grocery bag, and looked at it fondly. She had a real reader, and plenty of real homework that she could complete without help.

"Coming!" she called back.

Fifteen minutes later, she and her parents were pulling into the entrance to Marquand Park. Francie waved out the window to her best friend.

The four doors of the Nobles' station wagon opened all at once, and out climbed Kaycee, her older brother, George, and their parents.

"Ah, the perfect autumn day, Denise," Dana said to Kaycee's mother.

Francie stood still and breathed in deeply. She could smell fallen leaves and wood smoke. The trees in the park smoldered orange and golden and scarlet. The air was chilly, just chilly enough for sweatshirts, and Francie and Kaycee had agreed to wear their matching sweatshirts, the ones that said LEWISPORT, MAINE across the fronts.

"We're twins!" Francie exclaimed, even though she and Kaycee looked nothing alike. (Francie was slightly jealous of Dana, who actually was an identical twin.)

George Noble ran ahead of everyone, down a paved path through the park in the direction of the ball field. Francie watched him. George was two years older than Kaycee, and his legs looked impossibly long and skinny. It was like watching someone run on stilts.

"Play ball!" George called from the pitcher's mound on the baseball diamond. He smacked a baseball into his palm.

Francie was pleased to see that the ball field was deserted. They could have their very own baseball game on a real diamond.

"Nobles versus Goldbergs!" cried Kaycee.

"No fair!" Francie protested. "There are more of you."

"How about kids versus adults?" suggested George.

Kaycee considered this. "But there are only three of us, and four adults."

"Yeah, but we play better. Have you ever seen my dad run?" asked Francie. "Look, he isn't even wearing sneakers. We're way faster than he is."

"Okay. Kids versus adults!" called Kaycee.

George appointed himself pitcher for the kids, and he threw the first pitch to Dana, who hit the ball with a loud thwack, causing Francie's eyes to widen before she made a dash into the outfield.

"Surprised?" panted Dana as she rounded home plate several moments before Francie threw the ball to Kaycee.

"Adults, one; kids, zero!" Kaycee's father declared.

The game continued until a group of children who were at the park for a birthday party showed up with their bats and balls and asked if they could play.

"Sure," said Mrs. Noble. "I think it's time for us to stop anyway."

"That's 'cause you're still beating us," said Kaycee, but she was smiling. "Come on, Francie. Let's go to the Fairy Tree."

The tree that Francie and Kaycee had named the Fairy Tree (they had now forgotten why) was nearly a hundred and fifty years old. They liked to lie under its ancient branches, look to the sky, and imagine a world that was a hundred and fifty years younger.

"Are you girls just going to lie there and make up stories?" George called as they ran along a path toward the tree.

"Yes," Kaycee replied.

"Boring." George and his father and Matthew walked off in the direction of the arboretum, while Dana and Mrs. Noble began to unpack the picnic baskets they'd brought.

"A hundred and fifty years ago," Kaycee began as she and Francie settled themselves on the ground beneath the Fairy Tree, "do you think we would have been best friends?"

"Did they have best friends a hundred and fifty years ago?" asked Francie.

"Well, let's say they did."

"Did we get to go to school together?"

"Yes. In a one-room schoolhouse."

"But we could only go to school when we weren't working on our farms," added Francie.

"What kind of farms did we have?"

"Pig farms."

"Both of us?"

"Yes. Jed, too. Only his pigs smelled worse, which meant Jed smelled worse, so at school the kids called him Hog Boy. And even though Jed was very mean to us all day long, we stuck up for him. He never said thank you, but we knew he meant to. The end."

Kaycee grinned. "Make up another story about when we lived in Princeton in eighteen twenty-eight."

"Hmm," said Francie. "Okay. Well, the teacher in our one-room schoolhouse was Mrs. Pownell. And one day, Jed came to school with a flying squirrel in his lunch pail. A live flying squirrel, and —"

"Kaycee! Francie!" George called from across the park. "Lunch is ready. Come on!"

"Food!" cried Francie. "I'm starved."

The girls heaved themselves up from the ground and ran to the picnic tables. "Hey, there are a lot of people here now," Francie observed, looking around at laden tables and laughing families. She sat down at the table on which Kaycee's mother was setting out napkins and paper cups while Dana unwrapped a platter of sandwiches. Kaycee slid onto the bench next to Francie, and soon everyone was talking and laughing and filling their plates.

"Yum! Pickles!" said Francie, reaching for one.

George was setting three entire sandwiches on his plate and Kaycee was asking her mother if she could have dessert first when Francie noticed an older couple who had sat down at the table next to theirs. They were watching the Nobles — and the man was shaking his head in disgust.

"Let's move," the woman said. "We don't have to eat here."

Francie set her sandwich down and looked at Dana. "Why are they leaving?" she whispered. "What's wrong?"

"We're wrong," Kaycee's father said loudly.

"Richie," said Mrs. Noble, putting her hand on his arm.

He shook it off. "They're upset," he continued, just as loudly, "because I'm white and Denise is black, and we had the *audacity* to get married and have kids." He turned to the couple, who were now no longer looking at the Nobles.

Francie turned to her parents, frowning.

"That's bad?" she asked. "It's bad when one parent is one thing and the other is something else?"

"No, of course it isn't bad," said Matthew.

"Huh," said Francie. She stood up and glared at the couple. "Maybe you should get all mad at my family, too. My father is Jewish and my mother is Presbyterian. Is that a problem for you?"

"Francie," said Dana warningly.

Francie ignored her mother. "I hope you two are *exactly* the same," she said to the couple, who were now stuffing things into their picnic basket in a big hurry. "Oh no, wait, you're not. You'd better be careful. Someone might hate you because you have gray hair," she said to the man, "and you have . . ." She hesitated as she studied the woman. ". . . blue hair."

The woman shot Francie a furious look as they struggled off the benches and stalked away.

"Francie!" exclaimed Matthew. "Where did that come from?"

"Am I in trouble?" she asked.

There was a long pause. Then Kaycee's father began to laugh. "You certainly put them in their place," he said.

"That was great!" cried George.

"A little over the top," said Dana, who didn't look mad at all. "But no worse than something I once said to a grown-up who was rude to your uncle Peter."

"My uncle Peter has Down syndrome," Francie informed the Nobles.

"Can we eat now?" asked George.

"Watch how much he eats," Kaycee whispered to Francie.

The incident largely forgotten, Francie watched, awe-struck, as George Noble ate the three sandwiches and one and a half more, plus two apples and three helpings of macaroni salad, washed down with a quart of milk.

Later, when the picnic was finished and the Goldbergs and Nobles were walking back to their cars, Francie took her mother's hand. "We have to stick up for ourselves, don't we?" she said. "We have to say what we believe in."

"Absolutely," replied Dana.

Chapter 4

Francie sat up in her bed at the beach cottage in Maine. She leaned back against her pillow and looked across the room at the mirror over the dresser. Reflected in it, she could see her bed-rumpled head — a tangle of hair falling over pale cheeks. She had inherited her father's eyes and her mother's fair complexion. Francie and Dana never ventured onto the beach across the street without first slathering themselves with sunblock.

A second head was reflected in the mirror, and it belonged to Kaycee. Her hair, as wild as Francie's but longer and cocoa brown, was fanned across her pillow. Her eyes, which were still closed, were an interesting shade of hazel, a shade Kaycee detested. "They aren't brown, they aren't black, they aren't green, they aren't anything!" she'd once wailed.

"Of course they're something," Francie had replied. "Everything is *some* color."

"You don't have to be so practical."

"Let's come up with a nice name for the color of your eyes. How about caramel?"

"Hmm," Kaycee had said. "They are sort of caramelish."

"And you do like caramel," Francie pointed out.

So the girls had decided that Kaycee had caramel eyes.

Francie turned now to look at Kaycee, who was sleeping soundly, even though sunlight was filtering into the room. Then she sat up on her knees and peered out the window. Below her was Blue Harbor Lane, across from that was a narrow strip of beach, and beyond the beach stretched the great green Atlantic Ocean, which was an icy temperature, even at this time of summer.

Francie thought of other mornings she had woken up in this bed. She thought of all the mornings her Grandma Abby had woken up in this bed. This bedroom, this teensy room in this teensy house, had once belonged to Grandma Abby and her sister, Francie's great-aunt Rose. They had grown up here in Lewisport, Maine, at least until they were young girls. Then they had moved to a grand house in Barnegat Point.

Francie turned back to Kaycee and nudged her shoulder.

Kaycee didn't move.

"Kaycee?" Francie whispered.

"Mmphh."

"Come on, wake up."

"Okay."

"I mean, *now*."

"No. I have to wake up slowly." Kaycee absolutely could not be rushed in the morning.

"Don't you want to go to the beach? I want to show you the beach and the places Dana talks about —"

"First, tell me about your family — all the people I'm going to meet at the party this afternoon. I promise I'll open my eyes while you're talking."

Francie heaved a great sigh. "Okay. But I'll start with the people you *aren't* going to meet. You aren't going to meet my mom's grandfather. He's the one everyone calls Papa Luther, and he's sort of like the head of the family. Dana says the idea of a family having a head, especially a male head, is too old-fashioned, but whatever. And you aren't going to meet his wife, Helen."

Kaycee, whose eyes were still closed, asked, "You just call her Helen? Not Mama Helen or Great-Grandma Helen?"

"Yup, just Helen. She's his second wife."

"So she's, what? Your mom's step-grandmother?"

"I guess so. And you won't meet Luther and Helen's son, Miles, or any of Miles's family."

36

"And why won't I meet all these people?"

"Because Papa Luther and Helen don't like Matthew, so none of them are coming to the party."

Kaycee opened her eyes. "Why don't they like Matthew?"

"Because he's Jewish."

"So are you. Half Jewish anyway, and half . . . what's the other half again?"

"Presbyterian. But Papa Luther considers me Jewish like Matthew."

"So he doesn't like you either?"

Francie wove the fringe of the bedspread through her fingers. "Well, he kind of has to like me, at least a little, since I'm his great-granddaughter. But I guess he doesn't . . . *approve* of me."

"Huh. Since when do family members get to *approve* of other family members?"

Francie was trying to come up with an answer for this when Kaycee suddenly sat up, fully awake, and said, "Hey, what would this Papa Luther think of *me*?"

Francie flushed. "I guess he wouldn't approve of you either. But you don't have to worry about that because you and Matthew aren't coming with Dana and Adele and me when we visit him this afternoon."

"Good. I wouldn't want to visit him."

37

Francie made a face. "I don't want to visit him either. You know who he reminds me of? Remember those people we met at Marquand Park last year? The ones who were sitting at the picnic table next to ours?"

"Yeah," said Kaycee. And then, *"Oh."*

Francie nodded. "Adele says Papa Luther only likes people who are just like him — white and Christian. Not black or Asian. Not Catholic or Jewish. Not foreign."

"Do they have to be old and ugly, too?" asked Kaycee.

Francie snorted. Then she flopped back on her pillow. "It's not fair that I have to visit him this afternoon!" she moaned. "He makes me feel like I don't fit into my own family. Like there's something wrong with me."

"I'll bet it'll be a short visit. Don't think about it too much. Tell me about the rest of your relatives."

Francie brightened. "Okay. Well, Grandma Abby's middle sister is coming to the party. She's Dana's aunt and everyone calls her Aunt Rose. Her husband and kids and *their* kids are coming, too. Then there's Dana's twin sister, Julia, and her husband; Dana's sister Nell; and her brother, Peter. Uncle Peter's the one with Down syndrome. He lives with Grandma Abby and Orrin, who's Dana's stepfather, but they aren't coming to the party, so Aunt Rose is going to bring him."

"Why isn't your grandmother coming? Don't tell me she disapproves of you and Matthew, too."

Francie shook her head. "Nope, it's something to do with my mom. The two of them try to avoid seeing each other. They don't even speak to each other very much. I'm not sure why."

"Wow, there sure are a lot of people in your family who don't get along."

"I know," replied Francie. She was not proud of this fact. "But there are even more who do, so the party is going to be great. Tons of aunts and uncles and cousins. Lots of kids. Everyone here for a big picnic on the beach. I just have to get through the visit with Papa Luther and Helen first."

"You'll get through it. Come on," said Kaycee suddenly. "Let's go outside. Show me the beach. What are you waiting for, lazybones?"

Francie grinned. "You're the one who didn't want to be rushed."

She reached for the bottle of sunblock, and the girls threw on their bathing suits and ran downstairs. They found Dana, Matthew, and Adele sitting side by side on the front stoop, drinking coffee.

"Where are you two off to?" asked Matthew.

"The beach," Francie replied. "Can we go in the water?"

"At seven a.m.?" said Dana. Then she shrugged. "Sure. Why not? What's a vacation for? Don't go past your ankles, though. Not until one of us can come with you."

Francie turned her face to the morning sun. She breathed in the salty air and the scents of seaweed and wet sand. She could almost feel her hair becoming wavier in the damp morning. "Race you to the water!" she said to Kaycee. The girls dashed across Blue Harbor Lane to the rocks and sand beyond. "Isn't this the most perfect place?" she asked, arms flung wide. "I wish I lived here. You know, Dana lived here once."

"Really? I thought she grew up in New York." Kaycee scuffed through the chilly sand to the water's edge and let the ocean lap her toes.

"She did mostly, but after Dana's father died, Grandma Abby moved the family around a lot, and one of the towns they lived in was Lewisport, right here in the beach cottage."

"Would you *really* want to live here?" asked Kaycee. "Would you want to move here?"

Francie considered this. "Well, no. I just love visiting. Wait until we go into town. There's a bakery that sells the best donuts. Dana will probably get some for breakfast tomorrow. And I'll show you the school that Grandma Abby and

Adele and Aunt Rose went to. And the mini–golf course and the place where we buy lobsters." She paused, frowning. "But first, I have to visit Papa Luther."

Shortly after lunchtime, Francie, Dana, and Adele climbed into the Goldbergs' Ford station wagon and made the short drive to Barnegat Point. Francie chattered all the way out of Lewisport, but when Dana turned the car onto Haddon Road, she fell silent. Papa Luther's grand home loomed before them.

"I don't want to go in," Francie whispered. At her mother's insistence, she was wearing a sundress and had pulled her hair back with a pink ribbon.

"Neither do I," said Adele.

"Neither do I," said Dana. "But it's our duty. Besides, Papa Luther *is* your great-grandfather."

Francie was about to say, "So?" but she stopped herself.

Dana parked the car in the street. Francie took her mother's hand and the three of them walked along the white-pebbled driveway to the front porch.

"Maybe they won't be home," whispered Francie, but the door was opened by a housekeeper before Adele could even ring the bell.

The woman, who was short and stout, smiled warmly at them. "Come in, please," she said, and showed them to the living room.

Papa Luther and Helen were standing in front of the fireplace. Papa Luther was wearing a suit (with a jacket and tie in the middle of July, Francie noted with amazement) and Helen was wearing a rose-print dress. She smelled of powder and peppermint.

Francie looked first at her mother and then at Adele, who hesitated, then crossed the room and kissed Helen on the cheek. "It's good to see you," she said. She turned to her father. "Hi, Pop."

Francie let her mouth fall open. If *she* hadn't seen her father in a year, she would have wrapped her arms around him and not let go. She would have clung to him like an octopus.

"Adele," said Papa Luther.

Dana stepped forward. "Hello, everyone," she said nervously. She turned to Francie. "You remember Francie."

Francie hung back. The last time she had stood in this room, Papa Luther had studied her gravely, announced that she looked exactly like her father, and turned his attention back to Dana.

Francie waved a hand through the air. "Hi."

"Well, you've certainly grown," Helen said after a moment.

"What grade are you in now?" asked Papa Luther.

"I'll be in fourth. Um, and I like to write, just like —"

"So how's the book business?" Papa Luther asked Dana.

"Fine. I'll have a new book out this fall. Another picture book."

"Wonderful, wonderful. And the . . . costume business?" he asked Adele.

The awkward questioning continued for half an hour as the housekeeper brought tea (*hot* tea) to the living room and everyone sat on the very edges of their seats, balancing teacups, trying not to spill, and waiting for Papa Luther to get to his feet and end the visit.

An hour later, Francie burst through the door of the beach cottage to find Matthew and Kaycee in the kitchen, making deviled eggs for the party.

"It was awful!" Francie exclaimed. "Just awful! You guys are so lucky that you didn't have to go!"

"But now it's over," said Kaycee.

"And the party will start very soon. Come on, everyone," said Matthew. "Let's get things rolling."

The sun hung low over the ocean by the time Francie's relatives had arrived. She matched faces to names for

Kaycee's sake. She gave Aunt Rose a long hug and she squealed as she greeted each kid who arrived. She had long since given up trying to figure out whether the kids were second or third cousins, or cousins once removed. They were simply family.

Aunt Julia arrived with her husband, Keith, and Francie squealed (again) when she saw that Julia was going to have a baby. "Another cousin!" she exclaimed.

Suddenly, she noticed Peter standing quietly behind Aunt Rose. Francie wasn't sure it was all right to hug him. She did, though, and found herself locked in a bear hug as Peter said, "Hi, Francie. Hi, Francie, my niece."

Aunt Nell, who wasn't yet twenty and was a student at a college in Maine, arrived with her boyfriend. Then a pile of younger cousins arrived in a van. Before Francie knew it, a volleyball net had been set up on the beach, platters of food were being carried across the street, and the party was officially underway.

"Wow," said Kaycee under her breath. "This is amazing. You have an enormous family."

"Yeah," agreed Francie, who sometimes felt removed from these relatives she saw only once or twice a year.

The highlight of the evening was not the clambake, not the volleyball tournament (which Francie's team won), and not even the moment the sun set over the horizon. It was what happened shortly after Dana said, "Francie, go inside and get the story you wrote last week. I want you to read it to everyone."

Francie retrieved the story, read it aloud, her heart pounding, and then looked nervously at her relatives.

"Well, my goodness," Aunt Rose said at last. "Francie inherited Zander's talent. We have another writer in the family!"

Chapter 5

Francie sat at her desk in the second row of Mr. Apwell's fourth-grade class, wishing mightily that Kaycee were sitting next to her. This was the first year the girls had not wound up in the same classroom, and Francie missed her friend. On this day, her thoughts — which should have been on Mr. Apwell's lesson about amphibians — were on Halloween, and in particular on the costumes she and Kaycee had been creating. Francie was to be Elvis Presley and Kaycee was to be Donna Summer. They planned to go trick-or-treating with Amy Fox, who would be dressed as a fox. Francie had tried to convince her to dress as Michael Jackson, but Amy liked her fox suit.

Francie and her parents had worked hard on her costume. They had studied photos of Elvis, purchased an Elvis wig, and all three had spent hours making a blue-and-white rhinestone-studded Elvis suit. Francie was wiggly with excitement. How would she possibly wait until the next night?

At the front of the classroom, Mr. Apwell was saying, "Among the properties of amphibians are . . ."

What Francie heard instead was Kaycee's voice, saying, "Maybe we'll get so much candy that we'll have to go home, dump out our bags, and start over." Francie thought longingly of her orange trick-or-treat bag and imagined it filled to the brim. Then she imagined herself dumping the candy on her bed and running gleefully outside with an empty bag, ready to continue trick-or-treating.

When the morning ended at last and the fourth graders filed through the halls to the lunchroom, Francie and Kaycee claimed seats at the end of a long table.

"We carved pumpkins last night," Francie said as she pulled an apple from her bag. "Matthew's pumpkin is a monster, Dana's is a cat, and mine is a regular jack-o'-lantern. Like from *Charlie Brown*, with triangle eyes and a grin with missing teeth. Then we roasted the pumpkin seeds and Dana's going to use them the next time she makes granola."

"I love Halloween," said Kaycee with a sigh. "How are we ever going to wait until it's time for trick-or-treating?"

Francie shook her head. "It's like waiting for your birthday. Or the last day of school."

"Maybe I'll win an award in the Halloween parade tomorrow. I mean, a *real* award, not one that says, *Best Witch,* when you're the only witch in the parade, or even worse, *Nice Try!* I want a blue ribbon for Overall Best Costume."

"You could win Best Monster!" called Jed from down the table. "But only if you go as Francie."

Francie rolled her eyes at Kaycee, and Kaycee called, "What's *your* brilliant costume, Jede*di*ah?"

"I'm going as Frankenstein."

Kaycee's mouth dropped open. "Seriously? Again? Isn't it time to try something new? Or do you just like dressing up as someone smarter than you?"

Jed took a large bite of his sandwich, chewed it, and turned to Kaycee and Francie, his mouth open wide. "Lookie!"

"Ew! Oh, disgusting!" cried Francie.

"Ignore, ignore," said Kaycee under her breath. "Let's go outside."

The girls ran for the swings, where they sat side by side, trailing back and forth, their minds on pumpkins and candy bars and parades.

"So here's the plan," said Francie. "You come over to my house at six o'clock tomorrow. It'll be dark by then. We'll go next door and get Amy and trick-or-treat in our neighborhood first. Then we'll get one of our parents to drive us over to your neighborhood and we'll keep going."

"Hey, where *is* Amy?" Kaycee asked suddenly. "I haven't seen her today."

"She's home with a cold. But her mother promised she could go with us tomorrow."

Francie sat on the swing and planned the rationing of her Halloween candy. With any luck, she could make it last until after Thanksgiving. She would separate all the candy bars first and put them in a bag. Then she would —

"Francie, Francie, Francie! Not wearing underpantsies!"

Francie glanced at the monkey bars, where Jed and Antoine were hanging upside down, chanting in unison. "You know," she said to Kaycee, "that used to bother me, but now I hardly hear it. They just sound like two annoying insects."

"Insects you'd want to swat," added Kaycee. She clapped her hands together and pantomimed wiping them off on her jeans. "Nice try, boys," she called over her shoulder as she and Francie slid off the swings.

When school finally dragged to an end that day, Francie shot up from her seat, grabbed her books and jacket, and ran out of school. For a moment, she stood uncertainly on the front lawn. She wasn't used to walking home without Amy. Not that she didn't know the way. Of course she knew the way. She'd been walking to school since kindergarten. She just wasn't used to walking alone.

She buttoned her jacket, hefted her book bag into her arms, and set out for Vandeventer Avenue. At first, she walked between other groups of kids on their way home. Then, one by one, the groups veered off onto side streets. Francie was vaguely aware that Jed was somewhere behind her, but she refused to turn around and look at him. She didn't want to give him the satisfaction.

She reached a corner and realized that she was now nearly alone on the street. But she had only one more corner to turn, then three more blocks, and she'd be on Vandeventer.

Francie envisioned her costume again. She thought of her wig and the sparkly white belt she and Matthew had worked on. As she was picturing the very tight pants she planned to wear, she became aware that a car, a black station wagon, was driving along beside her, moving very slowly.

She turned to look at the car. A man was at the wheel. He pulled the car to a stop, leaned across the passenger seat, rolled down the window, and said, "Hey, there!"

Francie paused. She pointed to herself. "Me?"

The man grinned at her. He was handsome and young, with neat brown hair that curled just a little around his ears, and green eyes that twinkled like Mr. Friedman's did when he told Francie a joke. But something about his smile made Francie take a step away from the car. It was as if an alligator were smiling at her.

"Of course I mean you!" the man said, widening his grin. "Your mom sent me to pick you up. She said she didn't want you walking home from school alone."

Francie stepped back to the car. She and Dana and Matthew had had a conversation at breakfast that morning about this very subject. Since Amy would be absent, Matthew had planned to walk Francie to school and then run an errand before he went to work. But Francie had begged to be allowed to walk home by herself, and her parents had finally consented.

Now she wondered if her mother had changed her mind.

"My mom called you?" she asked.

"Yup. So why don't you come on and get in the car? You can meet my puppy," the man added. He nodded toward the back, and when Francie cupped her hands and peered through the window, she could see a small black puppy — maybe a Lab? — tumbling across the seat with a rubber fireplug in its mouth.

The man laughed. "His name is Bubbles."

Still, Francie hesitated. If Dana had changed her mind, she would have called the school and sent a message to Mr.

Apwell, right? Francie was stepping away from the car again when the man's hand shot through the open front window and grabbed her wrist.

Francie gasped.

The man was strong, stronger than Francie could have imagined, and he jerked her against the side of the car.

Francie was struggling to pull away when, from somewhere behind her, she heard a shout. "Hey! Francie Goldberg!" This was followed by a laugh. And then she heard Jed chant, "Francie, Francie, Francie! Not wearing underpantsies!"

"Jed!" Francie shrieked, but he was already running off, trying to catch up with Antoine. It didn't matter. The man, startled, had loosened his grip, and Francie broke away from him.

A car turned onto the street then. Francie sucked in air, ready to scream, but no sound came out.

"So, your name is Francie Goldberg," said the man softly, glancing at the car. "That's a nice name. Francie Goldberg." He slid back to his spot behind the wheel and offered Francie another of his grins. Then he licked his lips. "Francie — Francie Goldberg," he sang. "Maybe you don't tell anyone what just happened here and I won't come find you." He drove off, smiling.

Francie stood on the sidewalk and watched the station wagon. This was exactly what her parents had been afraid of — that something would happen to her while she was on her own. She'd been given her independence and look what had happened.

Francie wanted to run, but her legs wouldn't move. She felt as if she were in the dream she sometimes had, in which she was lost in a nighttime forest and could hear something large crashing through the underbrush — but when she tried to run from whatever it was, her legs wouldn't work. She would wake up gasping, heart pounding.

Now, as she stood rooted to the sidewalk, her breath began to come fast until she was gulping air. The man knew her name. He could find her if he knew her name. It wouldn't be difficult. He could figure out what school she went to as well. There was only one elementary school in the neighborhood. He could wait and watch for her. He could follow her. Or he could find her at her home.

Just as bad, Francie had watched enough scary movies on television to know that she knew too much about the man. She could describe him. She could describe his car. Francie wanted to run after him and shout, "I won't say anything! I promise!"

But the car had disappeared from sight.

Francie thought of the man repeating her name. She tried to shake the image and the words from her head, and she began to run. But as her feet pounded the sidewalk, she heard the man's voice over and over again: "Francie Goldberg. That's a nice name. Francie Goldberg. That's a nice name."

Francie ran until she came to an intersection near her house, an intersection so big that a crossing guard was stationed there. She paused, out of breath, holding back tears.

"Everything all right?" the guard asked her.

Francie nodded. "Yup. I'm okay."

"You sure?"

"*Yes.*" Francie stopped herself from adding, "Leave me alone."

The guard waved her across the street and, a block later, Francie turned down Vandeventer. She paused and looked behind her to make sure the man wasn't following her, but saw only an aging blue Volkswagen bus and the little yellow car that belonged to the Newcomers.

Heart pounding, Francie ran down her street. She passed the Foxes' house and saw Amy at her bedroom window, waving to her. Francie lowered her head, picked up her pace, and flew across the lawn, bursting through her front door. Kaycee's mother and Dana were seated on the living room couch, drinking coffee.

"Francie! My goodness, is something wrong?" asked Dana. She set down her cup.

"No! Nothing!" Francie threw her book bag on the floor and ran up the stairs to her room. The man's face swam in front of her eyes. She wanted to take a bath, to wash the man away — this man who knew her name.

Behind her, she heard startled laughter and her mother's voice: "She's already becoming a teenager!"

Francie slammed her door shut and threw herself on the bed. She felt tears again, but before she allowed them to flow, she leaped to her feet once more and looked out her window at Vandeventer. She checked the cars on the street below. No black station wagons.

She lay down, pillow over her head, and tried to slow her breathing, but she eventually crept to her window again to check for black cars.

Francie checked the street fourteen times and took two baths before Dana called her for dinner.

Chapter 6

Monday, November 12th, 1979

Francie's morning routine — she liked routines — had changed in the past two weeks. Now it involved peeping through a gap in her curtains and looking down at Vandeventer in the early morning quiet exactly five times between when she first woke up and when she was finally dressed and ready to go downstairs. Even though she had not seen the black station wagon, not since that horrible day two weeks earlier, she still expected it to appear at any time. How long, she wondered, might it take for the man to find out where she lived? ("Francie — Francie Goldberg.")

Francie had tried to celebrate Halloween — to put on her costume and march in the parade at school, to trick-or-treat with Kaycee and Amy — while pretending that nothing was wrong. But soon everyone could tell that something was very wrong.

"You didn't sort your candy yet?" Amy had asked on the day after Halloween, when she'd spotted Francie's full bag of candy inside her closet, where she'd left it at the end of an uninspired night of trick-or-treating.

"You've barely eaten a thing in two days," Dana had said as she'd watched her daughter pick her way through another dinner that night. "Are you sure you're feeling all right?"

"Francie, how come you don't talk to me?" Kaycee had asked, lip trembling, on Friday morning as they'd entered school. "Did I do something wrong? Are we having a fight? Please tell me what I did."

"Francie? Any reason you didn't hand in your home-work?" Mr. Apwell had asked her a few minutes later. "You didn't hand in yesterday's work either."

She'd shaken her head. "I don't know," she'd muttered.

The truth was that, by Friday, Francie had actually been starting to feel just the teensiest bit better. There had been no sign of the car or the man or Bubbles. Not on Vandeventer and not anywhere on her route home from school.

Then had come the Friday night news.

Francie and her parents had settled themselves in front of the television in the living room after supper. Matthew had tuned the set to NBC, and Dana had exclaimed, "Hey, this story is from Princeton! Look — 'Developing story in Princeton, New Jersey.'"

Francie had leaned forward in her chair, breath catching

in her chest. That afternoon, a girl in Princeton, Erin Mulligan, a third grader at Riverside Elementary, had been abducted on her way home from school. She'd been walking by herself when two of her classmates, lagging behind, had spotted her getting into a car that pulled up alongside her.

"She just got right in the car!" one of the girls told a newscaster. "Like she knew the driver. We couldn't see who was driving, but we thought it was her mother."

The TV camera then focused on a reporter, a young woman standing on a street corner in a Princeton neighborhood, a small home lit up brightly behind her, police cruisers jamming the driveway.

"Now," said the reporter, "it's been made abundantly clear that the driver of the car was not Erin's mother, but an abductor. Mrs. Mulligan was at her house, waiting for Erin to come home from school. When Erin was an hour late, her mother began phoning her friends, and that was when she learned about the car. The police are calling this a kidnapping. According to the witnesses, the abductor was driving a black station wagon. If anyone has —"

Matthew had switched off the TV, glancing at Francie. "Pretty scary, huh?"

Francie nodded.

"You know better than to get in a car with a stranger, don't you? We've talked about this."

Another nod. Then Francie had gotten to her feet and crept upstairs to her room. She'd sat down very, very carefully on her bed, for some reason not wanting to wrinkle the spread. She'd stared at the closed curtains in front of her windows. If, she thought, she had told her parents what had happened to her on Tuesday — about the man and the car and Bubbles — maybe Erin would be at home with her own parents this very moment. But Francie had been afraid to tell. The man had made her feel scared. He had threatened her. He knew her name. He said he might come after her. Besides, if Francie told now, her parents would be angry that she hadn't told earlier. Very angry. And what about Erin Mulligan's parents? How angry would they be?

Francie had lain down on her bed and fallen asleep, and hadn't wakened until the morning, when she'd changed her clothes groggily and made her way downstairs to the kitchen. There, she had found Dana and Matthew at the breakfast table, listening to the news on WHWH, the local radio station.

"What —" Francie had started to ask, but Dana had held her finger to her lips.

"We're asking for volunteers," the newscaster was saying, "to help with search efforts. The police plan to comb the woods and streets of Princeton and surrounding areas for any sign of Erin Mulligan."

Dana had switched off the radio then.

"They haven't found her?" Francie whispered.

Dana shook her head.

"This doesn't look good," Matthew added.

"Don't say that!" Dana had exclaimed. "There's always hope. She hasn't even been missing for twenty-four hours yet."

The search for Erin — hundreds of volunteers walking through woods and fields, police officers searching houses — had lasted for days. At the end of each day, people would ask one another, "Is there any news? Did anyone find anything?"

The answer was always no.

For days, the answer was no.

Then came the morning of November 12th. Francie got dressed for school. When she was ready to face the day, she parted her curtains, checked the street one final time, satisfied herself that Vandeventer was clear of black station wagons, and made her way downstairs. She entered the kitchen just as her mother was switching off the radio.

"Well," said Dana grimly, "it's over."

"What is?" asked Francie. "What's over?"

"The search for Erin. They've called it off."

Francie slid into her place at the table and sat very still, her hands folded in her lap. "Did they find her?" she asked after a moment.

She saw her mother glance at her father.

Matthew, who was sitting across from Francie, his hair messy — his eyebrows messy, too, she noticed — said, "No. They called off the search because they don't think they're going to find her now. Not alive anyway."

"Matthew!" said Dana.

"Well, it's the truth. People are going to be talking about it today, and I'd rather Francie hear it from us." He looked across the table at her. "Do you have any questions about this?"

Francie couldn't speak.

There had been so many moments during the last two weeks when she had almost — almost — told her parents about the man. But she hadn't been able to bring herself to say a word. The man was a monster. He was a killer, maybe, and he knew Francie's name. "Maybe you don't tell anyone what just happened here and I won't come find you," he'd said.

She couldn't tell on him.

This morning, the search had ended and Erin hadn't been found. Francie certainly couldn't say anything *now*. It was way, way too late. She would be the girl who could have saved Erin, if only she'd spoken up. She would be almost as horrible as the man.

Francie straightened her back. She was aware that her parents were waiting for her to answer Matthew's question. "We have two quizzes today," she announced. "I studied really hard for them."

"I'm sure you did, sweetie," said Dana, frowning. But then she smiled. "Ready for breakfast?"

She filled Francie's plate and Francie cleaned it.

"You have your appetite back," Matthew commented.

"Yes," said Francie, who hadn't been hungry at all.

Francie walked to school that morning with Amy, who dawdled and wanted to show her some outfits she'd been designing. But Francie hurried her along. "We don't want to be late," she said.

She was sitting at her seat in her classroom, hands folded, her homework placed in the exact center of her desk, when the morning bell rang and Mr. Apwell closed the door and picked up his attendance book.

The morning marched on. Francie took a spelling quiz and

thought she had spelled every word correctly. (She had checked and rechecked her work, just like Mrs. Pownell taught her to do, and she had even traced the words with her finger, a trick she'd learned recently that helped her decide whether the words "felt" right.) She volunteered to take a folder of papers to the principal's office for Mr. Apwell. She cleaned out the pencil sharpener at the back of the room without being asked, and helped Jed when he had trouble with a math problem.

"Francie, you've been a model student this morning," Mr. Apwell said as she and her classmates lined up to go to the cafeteria.

"Thank you," she replied. She noted that her stomach felt strangely full, but she ate the entire lunch that Matthew had packed for her.

On the playground, Francie and Kaycee were watching a game of kick ball when Francie saw Antoine grab a fifth grader by the shoulders and give him a shove. "No fair!" Antoine shouted. "That was out and you know it. Wasn't it out, Jake? Wasn't it?"

"Definitely out," said Jake.

"It was not!" cried the older boy. He straightened himself and approached Antoine. Two of his friends stepped up behind him.

"You guys!" Francie called.

The boys turned to look at her, surprise on their faces.

"Don't fight. Seriously," said Francie. "Mr. Apwell is watching. So why don't you just have a do-over? Quickly, before Mr. Apwell decides to see what's going on."

Antoine and the boy looked at each other, then at Mr. Apwell.

"Do-over?" asked Antoine.

"Okay."

At dinner that evening, Francie and her parents were seated around the kitchen table. Francie ate an entire chicken leg before she realized that nobody had spoken since they'd sat down.

"What's wrong?" she asked her parents.

"Nothing," they replied.

The silence continued.

Finally, Dana said, "All I ask for is a little advance notice. Don't spring these things on me." She appeared to be talking to her plate.

"I *am* giving you notice," said Matthew. "The event isn't until tomorrow night."

Dana raised her head and looked directly at her husband. "Twenty-four hours is hardly advance notice. How long have you known about this?"

"Three weeks." Matthew let out a sigh. "I'm sorry. I forgot to tell you."

Dana rolled her eyes.

"Are you guys fighting?" asked Francie.

"No," said Matthew.

"Yes," said Dana.

"I got a one hundred on the spelling quiz and a ninety-nine on the social studies quiz," said Francie.

"That's great," Matthew told her. "Really. You're doing so well this year."

"Thank you." Francie turned to her mother. "You know what you should wear tomorrow? To whatever the event is? That blue dress and your paisley scarf. You look gorgeous in that outfit. Doesn't she look beautiful in it, Matthew?"

Matthew smiled hopefully at Dana, and after a moment, she smiled back at him. "But for the future," she said, still smiling, "twenty-four hours is not considered advance notice."

"Duly noted," said Matthew.

Francie looked from her mother to her father. She let out a sigh.

That night, she fell into bed, exhausted.

Chapter 7

Francie awakened in predawn darkness to hear something moving across the wood floor of her room. *Click, click, click.* She lay perfectly still and listened. She could hear breathing, too. Very quiet breathing. She rolled over in bed and tried to stare through the darkness. The movement (footsteps?) stopped and the breathing grew louder.

Trembling, Francie reached for the flashlight she kept by her bed, and her hand collided with something furry. She heard a yelp.

"Sadie!" Francie exclaimed. "I'm sorry." She set the flashlight down and switched on her reading lamp. "I thought you were downstairs."

A small golden dog jumped onto the bed and curled herself against Francie. Francie turned the light off and gathered Sadie into her arms. "Don't do that again," she whispered. "Don't sneak up on me."

When the alarm clock rang an hour later, Sadie was still curled into Francie, and Francie watched her sleep, eyelids twitching, paws flicking. "She's chasing rabbits in her dreams," Dana would say, although Francie wasn't sure Sadie had ever seen a rabbit.

Francie slid out of her bed and dressed quickly in the outfit she'd chosen the evening before. Today was special and she wanted to look just right. She would be standing before all the students in her school at one time or another that day.

She heard a gentle knock and turned to see her mother standing in the doorway. "Look at you two," Dana said softly.

Francie smiled. "Sadie snuck in here this morning."

"She looks pretty cozy."

"You know what I was thinking? It's almost Sadie's birthday. Her adoption papers say June tenth. I know we don't know *exactly* when she was born, but I think we should have a birthday party for her next month."

"A dog birthday party," said Dana. "I like that idea."

"It could be an adoption party, too. Six months since adoption day."

Francie still couldn't believe that Sadie had joined their family. She hadn't asked Dana and Matthew for a dog. She hadn't even been thinking about wanting a dog, not the way she used to yearn for a dog when she was younger. Then, one evening, early in December, less than a month after the search for Erin Mulligan had been called off, Francie's parents, looking serious, had asked her to join them in the living room.

"Am I in trouble?" Francie had wanted to know. She'd been working so hard to be the perfect daughter, the perfect student, the perfect friend that she could think of absolutely nothing she'd done wrong.

Dana and Matthew had actually laughed at this.

"Of course not," Dana had said.

"We have a surprise for you," Matthew added.

"What would you think —" Dana began, sounding very much as if she and Matthew had rehearsed this conversation.

"If we got —" Matthew continued.

"A dog!" Dana and Matthew said in unison.

"A dog?" Francie had exclaimed. "Really?"

"Really and truly," said Dana.

"What, for Hanukkah?"

"Nope. Not for any occasion," Matthew replied. "Just because."

Dana had grown serious. "You've seemed sad lately, honey. And you haven't been spending as much time with Kaycee and Amy as usual."

"But we're still friends," Francie had assured her quickly.

"Okay, good. That's good. But when you're at home, you seem lonely."

"And sad," added Matthew. "Like your mom said. We know it isn't easy being an only child."

"So we thought you'd like some company."

"Some nice dog company. There's nothing like the company of a dog. What do you say?"

"Yes! Oh yes!" Francie had jumped up and hugged her parents.

The very next day, they had driven to the animal shelter at the edge of town and, after a conversation with a friendly woman at the reception desk, a volunteer had led them down aisles of cages, each holding a dog needing a home. They saw large dogs and small dogs, old dogs and puppies, dogs that frantically tried to stick their noses through the wire mesh in their desperation to be petted, and dogs that plastered themselves against the backs of the cages and wouldn't look at Francie or her parents.

Only one dog attracted Francie's attention. She was small and golden, of uncertain background.

"I like her," Francie had told Dana and Matthew. The dog was sitting at the front of her cage, looking hopefully at Francie, her tail sweeping the ground behind her.

"What's her story?" Dana had asked the volunteer.

"Well," the young man replied, "she's about six months old. She came here last week. Someone rescued her from a lumberyard, where she'd been living with several other dogs. But I don't think she'd been on her own for very long. She's too tame and too sweet. She has a wonderful personality. A bit shy, but I don't think that will last."

Three days later, Sadie had joined the Goldberg family.

"Her name at the shelter was Angela," Francie had told Kaycee and George, who dropped by to meet Sadie the day she came home, and were sitting on the floor, petting her and whispering to her. "But I like *Sadie* better. She looks like a Sadie, don't you think?"

"What kind of dog is she?" asked George.

Francie had shrugged. "Maybe golden retriever and something else? She looks like a little, tiny golden retriever."

Sadie had fit into the family as if she'd always been part of it. Francie had snapped photos of her sitting beside the menorah, sitting under the Christmas tree, playing in the snow, pawing at a Valentine from George, and sniffing indifferently at an Easter egg. She'd begun a photo album for Sadie. She'd written stories about her, too, and then stories about lost dogs and homeless dogs and brave dogs.

Excellent work! Mr. Apwell would scrawl above Francie's compositions. *Well thought out. Very imaginative.*

The days following the unthinkable time of the man in the black station wagon had fallen away behind Francie. They'd turned into weeks and then months. Slowly, with Sadie at her side, Francie had begun to feel more like herself. People mentioned Erin Mulligan's name less and less often. It faded into the recesses of Francie's mind. Now fourth grade was almost over, and a day she'd been waiting for a very long time had arrived at last.

"Better get a move on," Dana said to her. "This is one time you certainly don't want to be late for school."

"I'm never late," Francie pointed out. "Besides, you don't want to be late either."

"Hey," said Francie as she and Dana turned into the school parking lot later that morning. "Today, you get to park in one of the visitor spaces. We're visitors! Well, you are."

Francie helped her mother unload boxes from the back-seat of the car. "Do you *promise* there are no embarrassing photos of me in here?" she asked as she lifted out the carton that she knew contained a slide carousel.

Dana smiled. "I promise. Except for that one of you standing naked at the front door."

"*WHAT?*"

"I'm kidding. There are a couple of cute ones of you — fully clothed — when you were younger, but that's it. There are also photos of Uncle Peter, Aunt Julia, Aunt Nell, and me when we were little. There are even a couple of photos of Adele and Aunt Rose and Grandma Abby when *they* were little."

"Why?" asked Francie. "What do all those pictures have to do with *Peter the Important*?"

"Well," said Dana, "you're probably going to hear me say this about a million times today, but most of my picture books are about my own experiences in some way. *Peter the Important* is based on the experience I had with your uncle in a New York City park when he was little — the time I stuck up for him when an adult was rude about his disability. I want to show your classmates that stories, whether they're long or short, can come from our own lives."

Francie walked proudly along the flagstone path and through the front doors of her school with Dana. They reported to the principal's office.

"And I didn't even do anything wrong," Francie said.

"As if," replied her mother. "You never do anything wrong."

Francie didn't answer.

* * *

From start to finish, this Thursday was different for Francie. She didn't set foot in her classroom until just before the final bell rang, instead spending the day with her mother; with Mr. Phelps, the principal; and with Ms. Clarke, a library aide who had volunteered to help Dana with her presentations.

"Not many authors have visited our school," Ms. Clarke commented later. "We're lucky to have you. The students will be fascinated to see how you work on your books."

Francie was standing on the stage in the auditorium, watching Ms. Clarke and her mother fiddle with the slide projector. An easel had been set up on the stage, along with two chairs, a microphone, and a small table holding colored markers.

Ms. Clarke checked her watch. "Ten minutes until the first presentation," she said.

"I think we're ready," Dana replied. "Francie? Are you ready?"

"I hope so." Francie was going to be onstage with Dana for all three presentations — the first one to the littlest kids, the next one to the second and third graders, and the final one to Francie's classmates and the fifth graders. Francie wished George could go to one of the assemblies, but he had moved on to middle school. He and Francie wouldn't be in the same school again until Francie started sixth grade.

Francie kept an eye on the hallway outside the auditorium. "They're here," she whispered to Dana a few minutes later. And before she knew it, she and her mother were standing in front of a sea of tiny faces. Francie felt butterflies take off in her stomach, but Dana stood calmly on the stage.

Later, after Mr. Phelps had greeted the students and introduced Dana and Francie, Dana sat on the stage and read *Peter the Important* while Francie helped her turn the pages. Then Dana presented the slides and talked about her family and where the ideas for her stories and pictures came from. She used the markers to demonstrate how she created characters. Finally, smiling, she asked the students if they had any questions for her or Francie.

A forest of hands began waving in the air. Dana called on a little boy, wearing overalls, who said, "I have a dog." Then she called on a little girl who said, "My father took the bus to New York today."

Ms. Clarke borrowed the microphone from Dana and said, "Does anyone have a question about writing stories or drawing pictures?"

There was silence until the boy in the overalls said, "Could you draw a picture of my dog?"

Later, as the students filed out of the auditorium, Dana said to Mr. Phelps, "Oh dear. Maybe the presentation was too grown-up for them."

But Mr. Phelps replied, "No, no. They loved it! I've never seen them so attentive."

The second presentation went better. When Dana asked for questions, hands flew into the air, and one after another, the students asked, "How do you know what makes a good story?" "How do you decide what to put in your pictures?" "When did you first start drawing?" There was even a question for Francie: "Do you like to write or draw, too?"

Francie could feel the butterflies again but she took the microphone from Dana and said, "I write stories all the time. Before I could write, I would tell stories to my parents. I guess we're a family of storytellers. My grandfather was an author, and my dad tells stories with his paintings."

Mr. Phelps and Ms. Clarke took Dana and Francie to the teachers' lounge for lunch then, and afterward, it was time for the final presentation — the one for the fourth and fifth graders.

The butterflies swarmed back into Francie's now-full stomach as she watched her classmates file into the auditorium. There was Kaycee. There were Jake and Jed and Antoine. And sitting with the fifth graders was Amy. Francie drew in a deep breath as her mother began her presentation for the last time. She kept a close eye on Jed, but he didn't move a muscle while Dana was speaking. When the presentation came to an end, he was the first to raise his hand.

"Watch out," Francie whispered to her mother.

"I just have a comment," Jed began, "and it's for Francie."

Francie couldn't believe that she was going to be accused, in front of all the fourth graders and all the fifth graders — and even the principal and her mother — of not wearing underpants.

"You're the best writer in our class," said Jed, face flushing.

"I — I —" stammered Francie, who had been about to reply, "I am too wearing underpants!" She glanced at her mother, then looked back at Jed. "Thank you," she said.

Other hands were raised.

"What does it feel like to have a famous mother?"

"How do you know when you've finished editing a story?"

"How do you remember your childhood so well?"

"Do people recognize you when you walk down the street?" (At this, Francie could hear Amy giggle.)

Hands were still raised when Ms. Clarke said, "I'm afraid we're going to have to stop. One more question and then it's time to go back to your rooms."

Later, Francie and her classmates walked through the halls while Dana and Ms. Clarke packed up the slides and supplies.

"This was quite a day for all of us," said Mr. Apwell when everyone had settled at their desks. "Francie, we're so glad your mother could talk to us. Students, there are only ten minutes left until the final bell. You may have free time until then."

Pandemonium followed. Squeals and laughter and shouting, until Mr. Apwell raised his hands and called for decorum. The shouting died down, but a fight broke out over a missing barrette. Francie suggested a search of the room and the barrette was located under a table, ending the fight. In the midst of this, Dana arrived.

"I wish I had twenty-two Francies in my class," Mr. Apwell murmured to her.

Francie, overhearing this, turned away. She banished the image of the man in the station wagon that had sprung into her head and instead began thinking of a story, a story called *Telling Tales*.

She began working on it as soon as she and Dana returned home.

Chapter 8

Thursday, November 27th, 1980

Francie stood in her bedroom, Sadie at her side, and breathed in deeply. "Do you smell that?" she asked Sadie. "It's turkey. You're going to smell that almost all day long. And you're going to get a bite of turkey at dinner. In fact, you'll probably get lots of treats today. This is your first Thanksgiving and everyone will want to spoil you."

Francie fastened a paper chrysanthemum to Sadie's collar and regarded her with satisfaction. "There. All ready for the holiday."

Downstairs, she found her father in the kitchen, fussing with dishes and foil-wrapped packages. The table and the counters were littered with serving utensils, plates, open bags of flour and sugar, wet dishcloths, open cookbooks, and several items Francie couldn't identify. Cheesecloth? A knife sharpener?

"Wow," Francie whispered to Sadie. "I hope you can find your water bowl."

She peeked into the dining room, which was considerably tidier, but was presided over by Dana, who was so nervous that she was talking to herself. "Oh no! We're missing a place card! . . . Wait, the napkins don't match!" She held a glass up to the light and turned it around, examining it. "The water glasses are spotty!"

"Um," said Francie from the doorway, "is today going to be fun?"

Her mother glanced up and smiled at her. Then she set the glass down and let out a breath. "Yes," she said. "It will be. I promise. I just want to make sure everything is perfect."

"It probably won't be *perfect*," Francie pointed out.

"And no one will expect it to be," said a voice from behind her.

Francie turned around and gave Adele a hug. "Thanksgiving is one of my favorite holidays," she announced, "whether it's perfect or not."

"Mine, too," Adele replied. "I love a big family gathering."

"Plus, it's the beginning of the whole holiday season," said Francie. "Next is Hanukkah, then Christmas, then New Year's Eve. And we'll get almost two weeks off from school." She turned to Dana. "What can I do to help?"

"Feed Sadie," her mother replied automatically, "and get dressed if you want to go to the Thanksgiving service at the chapel with Adele and me. We'll just have time for that before everyone arrives."

Francie managed to locate Sadie's dish and food in the kitchen disarray. On her way to her room to get dressed, she paused at the television and switched on the Macy's Thanksgiving Day parade. She remembered the year before, when she and Dana and Matthew had gone to New York City to spend the holiday with Adele. They had watched the parade in person then, standing on Central Park West in the chilly air, stamping their feet and blowing on their hands, eating hot chestnuts out of a paper bag. Afterward, they'd had Thanksgiving dinner at a restaurant, since Adele had never cooked a turkey in her life.

Francie's mind turned to other Thanksgivings. Two years ago, she and her parents had driven to Weston, New Jersey, to spend the holiday with Matthew's family. The year before that, they'd driven all the way to the beach cottage for a New England Thanksgiving. This year, the Goldbergs were hosting the holiday meal — seven guests if you counted Adele, who didn't seem like a guest at all.

Francie, heart pounding, switched off the television and ran to her room. The holiday season had begun.

*   *   *

University Chapel was a short walk from the Goldbergs' house. Francie, wearing a dress, her very first pair of panty hose, and a new pair of velvet-bowed black flats, felt far more grown-up than ten as she walked sedately between her mother and Adele in the direction of Nassau Street.

"I love the Thanksgiving service," she chattered. (She had been to it only twice before.) "My favorite part is the gospel choir. And the rabbi's talk two years ago was good. I wish Matthew could come with us."

"So do I," Dana replied. "But someone has to stay behind with the turkey." She turned to Adele. "Remember the year the turkey caught —" she began to say.

But Adele held up a finger, laughing. "Wait! Save all the stories for dinner. We'll have a storytelling feast."

"Yes!" exclaimed Francie.

Francie sat between her mother and Adele in the chapel and sang "Come, Ye Thankful People, Come." She listened to the rabbi and the priest; looked around at the joyful, hopeful faces; and before she knew it, the service was over and everyone was streaming back outside to the campus. Francie was home in time to see Santa Claus at the end of the parade.

"Are we ready? Are we really ready?" she heard her mother ask nervously as Francie switched off the TV.

Matthew put his arm around her. "We're ready. And it's a good thing, because my parents just drove up."

Francie flew to the front door and threw it open. "Hi!" she called. "Happy Thanksgiving!" She stood on the porch, Sadie bouncing up and down beside her, flower flopping, and watched Grandpa Arnold and Nonnie make their way up the walk. Twenty minutes later, the doorbell rang, Sadie erupted in barking, and Francie cried, "Everyone else is here!"

This time, she opened the door to her uncle David, who was Matthew's older brother, her aunt Serena, and her cousins Brian and Rachie. Rachie was exactly her age. They had been born on the very same day; although if you wanted to get technical, Rachie was three and a half hours older than Francie. Then there was Brian. Brian was four. Francie wanted desperately to like him, but he was what Adele called a Snatcher. As Francie held the door open for him, he lived up to this secret nickname by snatching the flower from Sadie's collar.

"Hey!" cried Francie. "Give —" Then she remembered herself. "Brian," she said gently, "that belongs to Sadie. She's really proud of it. This is her first Thanksgiving. Could you please give it back?"

Brian considered the flower in his fist before returning it to Francie, who reattached it to Sadie's collar.

The afternoon stretched ahead of Francie like the beach at Lewisport — glowing and full of promise. She and Rachie lay on her bed and whispered about cute boys. She showed Rachie and Brian the few unreliable tricks Sadie could do. She and her cousins joined the adults in the living room for hors d'oeuvres. Then finally — *finally* — Matthew announced that it was time for dinner.

"I'm starving!" cried the Snatcher, grabbing olives out of a dish before he had even settled into his seat at the table.

Francie ignored him. The meal began. No sooner had the guests been served and the food blessed when Adele asked, "Okay, what's everyone's favorite Thanksgiving memory?"

This was followed by silence, and then all at the same time, Dana said, "The year the turkey caught fire," Aunt Serena said, "The year of three Thanksgivings," Matthew said, "The year the stranger came," and Grandpa Arnold said, "Our very first Thanksgiving." He glanced at Nonnie.

"Your first Thanksgiving after you got married?" Francie wanted to know.

"Well, yes," Grandpa Arnold replied, "but what I meant —"

"I want to hear about the turkey on fire!" cried Brian.

"Don't interrupt, honey," Aunt Serena said softly.

Everyone turned to Grandpa Arnold. He cleared his throat. "Our very first Thanksgiving," he said. "Nonnie and I had just come to America, after the war."

"After the camps?" asked Rachie.

"Yes, after the camps. We met on the boat and we got married six months later. Everything in this country was new to us, even the language. We barely knew what Thanksgiving was, but we were certainly thankful to be here. Our first Thanksgiving was my favorite."

"Mine, too," said Nonnie, reaching for Grandpa Arnold's hand.

"Now tell about the turkey on fire!" said Brian.

Dana smiled. "Adele, you remember that Thanksgiving, don't you?"

"Of course."

"My family was still living in New York City then. I was about ten years old, and we were having what was supposed to be a formal Thanksgiving dinner at our house. But everything went wrong. First of all, there was a snowstorm. Then we couldn't find our cat."

"It turned out she was off having kittens," Adele explained.

"And somewhere in the confusion, the turkey caught fire and my father put it out with a fire extinguisher, so the guests were served bologna instead."

"Why did your father ruin the turkey?" Brian wanted to know.

"He didn't mean to. Sometimes he could be, well, impulsive," Dana said quietly. She gazed out the window for a moment, and Francie tensed. But then her mother's attention returned to the dining room and she said, "Adele, tell Grandma Abby's favorite Thanksgiving story, the one about the snowstorm."

The stories continued. Nonnie said, "Remember the summer Matthew thought he could fly?"

"I really did think I'd be able to fly if I tried hard enough," Francie's father replied. "Remember when Francie wanted a pet chicken?"

"Remember when I got in trouble for taking a toy home from school?" said Brian.

"Brian! That happened yesterday," exclaimed Rachie.

Adele let out a sigh. "It's sad that there are no stories about Fred."

Up and down the table, puzzled glances were exchanged. Finally, Francie asked, "Who's Fred?"

Adele frowned at her. "You don't know who Fred is?"

"No."

"He's my brother," Adele told her.

This was news to Francie. "You have a brother?"

"I most certainly do. Dana, you've never mentioned Fred to Francie?"

Dana shook her head. "I barely know anything about him myself."

"Fred is my older brother," said Adele, "although I hardly remember him. He was sent away when I was two."

"What do you mean, *sent away*?" asked Rachie.

Adele set down her fork, pushed her plate away, and began the story of the little boy — the only boy in a family of girls — who was supposed to be a source of pride for his father.

"For Papa Luther?" asked Francie.

"For Papa Luther," Adele said. "But something was the matter with Fred. He was slow. He didn't seem to be able to move properly. Eventually, he learned to sit up, but he didn't learn to walk and he could barely talk."

"What was wrong with him?" asked Rachie.

"I'm not sure what his diagnosis would be today, but back then, the doctors called him an imbecile and a cripple, and they convinced my father that he'd be better off in an institution. So one day, when Fred was four or five, Pop, without consulting anyone, including his wife, drove off with Fred and came back without him. He said he'd taken Fred to a special school, but I have a feeling Fred went somewhere very different. I've been thinking about him a lot lately."

No one spoke until Brian, looking impatient, said, "Uncle Matthew, you didn't tell us about the Thanksgiving stranger!" and the Thanksgiving stories began again.

But Francie still had questions. Lots of them.

That evening, after the guests had gone home and the kitchen had been cleaned up, Adele plopped down on a couch and set an old photo album in her lap.

"What's that?" asked Francie, sitting next to her. She rested her chin on Adele's shoulder.

"A family album. From when I was a little girl. There are a couple of pictures of Fred in here." Adele turned pages. Dana and Matthew joined them, sitting across from them on the love seat.

"I haven't thought of Fred in ages," said Dana. "I don't remember the last time anyone mentioned him."

"I don't think anyone has seen him since he left home," Adele replied, "except Pop. I have a feeling Pop checked in on Fred from time to time."

"Is Fred still in the institution?" asked Francie, appalled

at the thought. And then, before Adele could answer her, she said, "Are you sure he's even alive?"

Adele paused. "Well," she said at last, "no, I'm not sure. But I think he is. I think that if he had died, Pop would have said something about it." She set the photo album on the coffee table and pointed to a picture. Francie and her parents leaned in to look at it. "There's Fred," said Adele.

Francie saw a photo of two girls in white lacy dresses, posed on a sofa with a much younger boy between them. He looked as though he was supposed to be sitting up, but had tipped over just as the picture had been snapped. "Are the girls Grandma Abby and Aunt Rose?" asked Francie. Adele nodded. "Fred's head looks kind of . . ." Francie paused. "It looks like it's too big for his body. No offense, but he looks lopsided."

"He does look lopsided," agreed Adele.

"You really don't remember him?" Dana asked.

Adele shook her head and closed the album. Then she sat up very straight and announced, "I think it's high time we find Fred and make him part of our family again."

Dana looked at her, eyebrows raised.

"Fred is my brother," Adele went on. "He's a member of our family, but he seems like a secret."

"How do you think Papa Luther will feel about this?"

"I think he'll hate the idea."

Francie squirmed uncomfortably.

"But I think we should find Fred anyway," said Adele. "Besides, we're adults. Pop can't tell us what to do."

"No," said Dana slowly, "but we don't want to incur his wrath."

"I couldn't care less about Pop's wrath," Adele replied.

Sure enough, when the Goldbergs placed their Thanksgiving call to Papa Luther and Helen later, Adele boldly asked where Fred was. Papa Luther's reply was so loud that Francie hurriedly hung up the extension and retreated to her room. But when she joined the grown-ups later, Adele was smiling. "Pop told me the name of the place where Fred lives now," she said. "That's all he would tell me, but it's enough. Fred is alive and he's living in a town not too far from Barnegat Point. I plan to find him. He's going to be a member of our family from now on, not a secret."

"We'll help you," said Matthew.

"We'll *all* help you," added Francie. "It's the right thing to do."

Chapter 9

Friday, August 21st, 1981

"Sadie!" Francie called. "Sadie!"

Francie stood at the front door of the beach cottage in Lewisport and waited to hear the sound of Sadie's feet scrabbling across the kitchen floor. This was Sadie's second visit to Maine, and Francie had been able to tell, when they'd arrived at the cottage four days earlier, that Sadie remembered the house.

"And not just the house," she'd commented later to her parents, "but the beach, the sand, everything."

Dana had smiled. "She loved being here last summer."

"I think she was the happiest I'd ever seen her," Francie had replied. On her first trip across the street to the beach, Sadie had sniffed at the sand tentatively and reached out a paw. Next, she had investigated sea grass and rocks and shells, drawing ever closer to the water's edge. And then in one sudden burst of jubilation, she'd run up and down the beach, back and forth, back and forth, leaping and twisting, darting in and out of the ocean.

Then a year had gone by with no visit to Maine, and Francie had wondered if Sadie would remember the cottage when they returned. Luckily, she'd had the foresight to clip Sadie's leash to her collar before opening the car door when they arrived, since she was practically dragged across Blue Harbor Lane by an exuberant blond dog, eager to run on the beach again.

Now, four days later, their wonderful Maine vacation almost half over, Francie wanted to take an early morning walk on the beach with Sadie. "Before we get stuck in the car," she said to her as they crossed the street. "Today's an important day, you know."

Sadie had obliged happily, and she and Francie had returned to the cottage, sandy and out of breath, in time for breakfast with Dana, Matthew, and Adele.

"Big day," Dana said as Francie sat down at the table.

"That's what I was telling Sadie." Francie paused. "Are you sure it's okay if she comes with us?"

"I talked to the director twice and asked about Sadie both times, and she said it was fine. She said Fred likes dogs, and that Sadie might even help keep him calm."

Francie poured syrup over a stack of pancakes that Matthew set in front of her. "You must be nervous," she said to Adele. "Meeting a brother you don't even remember."

"I think we're all a little nervous," admitted Matthew.

Francie frowned. "If Fred is your brother, Adele, that means he's *your* uncle, right?" she said, turning to her mother. "And if he's your uncle, then is he my great-uncle?"

Dana nodded.

Francie chewed. "Does he know we're coming?"

"He's been told we're coming," Adele replied. "I'm not sure what that means to him. He's forty-nine years old and he doesn't know any of us. For all I know, he's not even aware we exist. I have no idea what Pop may have told him over the years. Probably nothing. And today he's going to meet his sisters, two brothers-in-law, a niece, her husband, and a great-niece."

"And a dog," added Francie.

"And a dog. I think he's going to be overwhelmed."

"I would be," said Matthew.

Privately, Francie herself was feeling somewhat overwhelmed. There was Fred, of course. A man who, as a child, had been called an imbecile and a cripple. She wasn't sure how she'd feel when she was standing before her great-uncle, who might still have the lopsided head, who might not even know how to talk.

Beyond that, there was Grandma Abby. She would visit Fred today, too, along with her husband, Aunt Rose, and Aunt Rose's husband. Francie loved her grandmother, although she hadn't spent much time with her. Her own mother did *not* get along with Grandma Abby, and this made Francie uneasy. She couldn't imagine not getting along with Dana.

As if she could read Francie's mind, Adele suddenly turned to Dana and said, "I hope you and your mother will behave yourselves today. Today is about Fred."

Dana made a face. "I am perfectly capable," she said stiffly, "of being in the same room with my mother and not making a scene."

"I hope so," murmured Adele.

Francie sat in the backseat of the Goldbergs' station wagon with her mother and Sadie, Sadie gazing seriously out the window, appearing to study the countryside as it rolled by, her wet nose making slimy prints on the window.

"Are we almost there?" Francie wanted to know. She had tried for miles to refrain from asking this question, but couldn't help herself any longer.

"Yup," said Adele from the front. "We're entering Bromton. Fred's group home is on the other side of town." She was holding a map in one hand and a page of written directions in the other.

"What *is* a group home?" asked Francie.

"Wait, I need to concentrate," Adele replied.

"It's a private residence for people with disabilities," Dana said quietly as Adele and Matthew navigated the crowded streets of Bromton. "A place that feels like a home instead of a school or an institution. Fred's home is for people with mental and physical disabilities. I think there are only seven other people living there besides Fred, plus the staff, who are there day and night. Fred has his own room. I don't know much more than that. Except that it must be very expensive. Papa Luther has been footing the bill for Fred's care for decades. He may have shoved Fred out of his life in a way none of us ever would have done, but at least he arranged for him to have good care."

"Eventually," Adele called over her shoulder. "Fred's first 'home' *was* an institution."

Francie shuddered.

"Well, here we are," Matthew said a few minutes later. He turned into a small parking lot by a sprawling Victorian house.

Francie's stomach fluttered. "I'm scared," she whispered to Dana. "What if he doesn't like us? What if he doesn't want us here?"

Dana offered her a smile and squeezed her hand. "I don't know, honey. We'll just have to see what happens. If things don't go well, we'll leave. We don't want to upset Fred."

Francie climbed out of the car, Sadie at her heels, and gazed at the building. "It looks sort of like Papa Luther's house," she said. And it did, except for a wooden sign by the front door that read WINGS.

"Huh," said Dana, peering at the sign. "Funny. That was the name of the first school Peter went to. He loved that school."

"Hey, here comes everyone else," Francie exclaimed as a car pulled into the lot and parked beside them.

Out stepped Grandma Abby and her husband, Orrin, and Aunt Rose and Uncle Harry. Francie hugged the new arrivals and then hung back and eyed her mother and Grandma Abby warily. Each gave the other a wordless peck on the cheek. That was all. They seemed to be behaving themselves. Grandma Abby turned to Francie, then wrapped her in a hug and held her close, patting her on the back and (Francie thought) trying not to cry. At last, she clapped her hands together and said, "Well! I suppose we should go on in." She looped her arm through her husband's and led the way resolutely along the walk to the front door of Wings. Francie led Sadie up the wheelchair ramp, just for the fun of it.

Orrin rang the doorbell and Francie's family waited, motionless and silent. Francie's heart began to pound.

The door was opened by a short woman with a round face and eyes that reminded Francie of her uncle Peter's. "Are you here to see Fred?" she asked. When Grandma Abby said that they were, the woman grinned. "My name is Amanda," she told them. "Won't you come in? I have door duty today. That's my job." She held the front door open while Francie, heart still pounding, filed inside with her family.

"Hey, it looks just like a regular house!" she couldn't help whispering to her father. She was standing in a large living room with a fireplace and chairs and couches, books and balls of yarn and sneakers strewn around, just like in Francie's own living room in New Jersey. A hallway led to the back of the house and Francie could see a kitchen at the end. To her right, a staircase led upstairs. The only unusual feature of the house was an elevator next to the staircase.

"Matthew! An eleva —"

But Matthew nudged Francie as Amanda began speaking again. She stood in front of the visitors, hands clasped neatly in front of her. "Please wait a moment while I get Fred. He's in the kitchen." She looked at Francie and added, "May I pat your dog?" After Francie said yes, Amanda gave Sadie a pat on the head and then hurried importantly in the direction of the kitchen. Several moments later, she returned, pushing a wheelchair.

Francie Goldberg found herself looking at her great-uncle Fred for the first time. She knew she shouldn't have been surprised to see a gray-haired man in the wheelchair, but since her only other glimpse of Fred had been in old photos, she'd half expected to see a little boy. The man, slumped in the chair, had thinning hair that was indeed beginning to turn gray, stubble on his chin, and hands that were spotted and wrinkled like Adele's.

For a moment, no one spoke. Amanda tactfully retreated to the kitchen.

At last, Grandma Abby stepped forward. "Fred? I'm Abby, your sister. Your big sister," she added in a trembling voice. "Do you remember me?"

"You're Abby, my big sister," Fred repeated. Francie thought he sounded like a mechanical toy.

"And I'm Rose, your other big sister," said Aunt Rose. She reached out a hand and almost touched the sleeve of Fred's shirt, but then drew back, and clutched Grandma Abby's elbow.

Adele glanced at her older sisters before she approached the wheelchair. "I'm your little sister, but I'm afraid I don't remember you," she admitted. Now Fred smiled. "Is it okay to give you a hug?"

"Oh no. Not a hug. Not yet," said Fred.

Adele stepped back hastily. "Sorry, sorry," she said. She reached for Grandma Abby's other elbow so that the three sisters were standing in a united but anxious row.

"I know this is a lot to take in," Grandma Abby went on. "We hope we're not too much for you, but we —" She hesitated and looked helplessly at the other members of the family. "But we wanted to get to know you."

"We've wanted that for a long time," added Adele, "except we didn't know where you were."

Again, no one spoke. So Francie, trembling, stepped forward, Sadie in tow. "I'm your great-niece," she said, and slipped her hand into Fred's. "My name is Francie. I'm really happy we found you."

Fred offered her a wide, slow grin, even as Francie noticed tears in his eyes.

"I don't know if you wanted a big family, but you've got one now," she added.

"I want a family," said Fred simply.

"Good," said Francie, "because there are more of us." She smiled. "A lot more. We didn't think we should all come at once, though."

"No," said Fred. "This is good." He struggled to sit up straighter. Then he shifted his attention to Sadie. "Is that your dog?"

Francie nodded. "Sadie. We rescued her from the shelter."

Fred's eyes lit up. "Tim has a rescue dog!" he exclaimed.

"Who's Tim?" asked Dana gently. "I'm Dana, by the way — your niece. I'm Abby's daughter."

Francie saw Grandma Abby's eyes flick to Dana, but Dana looked only at Fred.

"Tim takes care of me," said Fred. "We're helping out in the kitchen this morning."

Francie glanced up and noticed a man standing just outside the doorway, quietly keeping his eye on things in the living room. She gave him a wave and he waved back.

One by one, the members of Francie's family relaxed and sat down. From their purses and pockets, they pulled photos that they shared with Fred. They told him stories and answered his questions and asked questions of their own.

"Do you like living at Wings?" Francie wanted to know.

Fred nodded enthusiastically. "I love it. We play checkers. I can play checkers, you know. Does anyone want to play checkers?"

"I'll play with you," said Francie, "but I'm not much good."

While Fred found the checkerboard, Grandma Abby and Aunt Rose disappeared outside. When they returned, they held a whispered conversation with Tim, and soon everyone except Fred, Francie, and Sadie had left the living room.

Fred beat Francie at three games of checkers in a row.

Francie shook her head. "Checkers is very hard for me," she said truthfully.

Fred patted her hand. "Don't worry."

At that moment, the sound of voices singing "Happy Birthday" burst in from the hall, causing Fred to jump. Into the living room walked the rest of the visitors, Aunt Rose holding a platter with a cake on it, and everyone else holding wrapped gifts.

Fred's eyes widened. "But it was already my birthday," he said. "My forty-ninth birthday. Two weeks ago was my forty-ninth birthday. We had a cake then."

"But *we* haven't celebrated your birthday," said Grandma Abby, smiling. "We have years of birthdays to make up for."

Francie tried to remember the last time Grandma Abby had phoned on Dana's birthday, and couldn't. She set the thought aside.

Adele cut the cake then, Matthew handed the slices around, and Francie helped Fred open his gifts — new shirts and socks, a photo album, copies of Dana's books.

Fred grinned mightily. But eventually he began to look tired.

"Would it be all right with you if we visited again?" Grandma Abby asked as they stood and began gathering their things. "Rose and I don't live far away. And you have plenty of other cousins and nieces and nephews here in Maine. They'll want to meet you, too."

"I like visits," said Fred.

"Would you like to come visit me at my house sometime?" she went on. "We'd love to have you."

At this, Fred appeared nervous. "Oh no, no. Oh no, thank you. This is my home. This is my home, of course. My room is upstairs. I didn't show you my room, but it's right up there, right up the elevator. This is my home," he repeated.

"Okay," said Aunt Rose quickly. "We understand. But we would like to visit you again."

Francie led Sadie to Fred's side. "I live in New Jersey," she told him, "but we'll be back next summer. I could bring

Sadie again then." For most of the visit, Sadie had lain next to Fred, resting her head on his feet.

"Good," said Fred. "Good."

"So we'll see you soon," Adele called later as they left Wings, Fred watching from the doorway in his wheelchair.

"We'll see you soon," he echoed.

Francie turned around for one last look and saw Fred smiling. As she watched, he tipped his head back to glance up at Tim, who had appeared behind him, and said, "That's my family."

Chapter 10

Francie swung her legs over the side of the little bed in Adele's apartment and looked around the room, which was dim in the early light of a winter morning. This had been her mother's bed during the four years when she'd lived with Adele. These had been the things her mother had seen when she'd awakened every morning in her aunt's tiny, quirky apartment.

Those four years had been very happy ones for Dana — and for Adele — but not for Grandma Abby, Francie had come to realize. Grandma Abby had felt abandoned by her daughter. "Why couldn't she understand," Dana had once said to Francie, "that I needed to be back in New York? My mother had moved us to Maine and we were just traipsing around from town to town. I couldn't stand it. I was miserable. All I wanted was New York City, the one place that felt like home. And that's what Adele offered me when she said I could come live with her. She gave me my home back."

Francie yawned and stood up. She crossed the room to peer out of a window. Two years had passed since Erin Mulligan had disappeared, and it was still Francie's habit to start her morning by checking the street for black station wagons, even in the middle of New York City. What she saw now, though, was snow. And even though it was Sunday, Francie couldn't help but feel the same surge of excitement she felt when she looked outside on a weekday morning, saw a world of white, and thrilled at the thought of a day off from school.

"Morning, honey," said Adele as she emerged from her small bedroom. "Ready for another day in the city?"

"It's snowing!" was Francie's excited response.

"Perfect for the rest of our Christmas adventure," said Adele.

Francie and her parents had arrived in New York on Friday night for a weekend of holiday activities. Christmas was just two weeks away and Hanukkah slightly more than one week away. Francie had begged to be allowed to bring Kaycee along, but it was Adele, during a pre-visit phone call, who had insisted on a family weekend. "Besides, if Kaycee came with you, one of you girls would wind up sleeping on the floor," she'd added.

"That would be okay," Francie had said hastily.

"But Sadie's going to stay with the Nobles while we're away, and Kaycee's looking forward to that," Matthew had argued.

Francie let the subject drop. She wasn't about to spoil a weekend in New York with Adele. Especially not when things were going so well. Almost four months had passed since the trip to Maine and the visit with Fred. Four months during which Francie and Kaycee had entered John Witherspoon Middle School as nervous but excited sixth graders. Francie had worried about being among the youngest students in a school in which the oldest students were turning fourteen and dating, and the girls were experimenting with makeup, wore bras, and had figures with noticeable curves. But the year had gotten off to a good start — partially due to Kaycee's brother, George. George was a popular eighth grader. He had seen to it that Francie and Kaycee were treated with the respect ordinarily reserved for his classmates, and Francie had basked in this. She knew it wouldn't last, though. When George graduated in May, he would leave the world of public school and enter a private high school. Two short years later, Kaycee would follow him, and Francie would face Princeton High on her own.

But that was in the future. At the moment, all was well in Francie's world. She liked her teachers, she was contributing short stories and essays to the school paper, and an editor at the *Princeton Packet* — the town newspaper! — had even asked her to write an article about her experience adopting Sadie from the shelter. The article was published, and she had felt famous.

Now the holidays had arrived and Francie and her parents were in the fabulous Big Apple for their long-anticipated family weekend. Dana and Matthew were staying at a hotel, and Francie was enjoying treasured moments with Adele.

Adele opened the refrigerator and surveyed the contents. Her kitchen was not a separate room, but an extension of the living room, a source of fascination for Francie. "Muffins all right for breakfast?" asked Adele.

"Perfect," said Francie. She waited to see if her aunt would offer her coffee again. She had offered it the day before, saying that Dana had been fourteen when she'd started drinking coffee, but Dana had been in the apartment at that moment and had put an end to things quickly.

"Eleven-year-olds do not drink coffee," she'd said. "Period. The end."

Adele did not offer it now. Francie didn't care. She had sampled it once and decided it tasted like dirt.

Francie and Adele sat on the couch and ate their muffins.

"What are we going to do today?" asked Francie, who thought it would be hard to top the day before, which had been spent shopping and looking at the holiday windows, followed by dinner at a restaurant so fancy that the waiters wore tuxedos.

"The Radio City Christmas show," Adele began. "Well, now it's called the *Radio City Christmas Spectacular*. That'll be in the afternoon. Then we'll go to Rumpelmayer's —"

"Yay!" exclaimed Francie.

"And before you leave, we'll see the tree at Rockefeller Center."

"Perfect," said Francie again. Everything was perfect — the muffins, the weekend.

She and Adele spent a lazy morning at the apartment. They finished their muffins, sat around in their pajamas, and talked. Francie regularly told Adele things that she shared with Kaycee but not with her parents.

"So . . . any cute boys in your grade this year?" Adele wanted to know.

Francie looked out the window at the snow, which continued to fall lazily. "A few. There are so many new kids in school, because kids from all the elementary schools go on to John Witherspoon, that it's a little hard to keep them straight. But there's this one boy? Anthony Neceda? We have two classes together — French and study hall — and he smiles at me a lot. There's going to be a Valentine's Day party at school and maybe he'll ask me to dance. I don't know . . ." Francie trailed off. This was new territory.

"What about Kaycee? Does she have a boyfriend?"

Francie giggled. "No! We're too young for actual boyfriends. But she likes Barry Garman, even though he hasn't noticed her yet."

Adele's buzzer sounded and she exclaimed, "Yikes! Here are your parents and we aren't even dressed yet!"

A few moments later, as Francie and Adele scrambled for their clothes, Dana and Matthew let themselves into the apartment. "Ah," said Dana, collapsing onto the daybed that Francie had been sleeping on. "Home sweet home."

"Are you going to say that *every* time you come in here?" asked Francie.

"Probably," said Dana. "I loved this place." Her eyes fell on the birdcage, with the leaves of a spider plant trailing through the bars. "That isn't the same plant that was in there when I lived here, is it?"

Adele laughed. "No. But it's one of the spider plant babies. Or maybe it's a grandchild."

Dana shook her head. "This apartment was heaven," she said rapturously.

*　　*　　*

Half an hour later, Francie and her parents and Adele set out through the streets of Manhattan. They scuffed along in the snow, Dana and Matthew in front, Francie and Adele behind them. Francie remembered when her parents used to hold hands. Now they kept them in their pockets, out of the cold and snow. Her parents were getting old, Francie decided, and she made a mental note that when she was married, she and her husband would always be romantic, even when they were ninety-two.

The snow continued to fall. They walked on, passing apartments with wreaths on the doors, shopwindows outlined in gold lights, and Christmas trees sparkling in building lobbies. They walked by stalls where trees were for sale, Christmas music playing loudly.

"Santa baby, a fifty-four convertible, too, light blue!" Francie sang along as they passed one stall.

Adele laughed. "Now, how do you know that old song?"

Francie shrugged, and Adele looped her arm through her great-niece's.

Dana turned around and called over her shoulder, "There's no place like New York City when you're in the Christmas spirit."

At Radio City, Francie and her family sat in the first row

of one of the balconies. They watched the Rockettes kick their legs high, and clapped when the dancing elves had finished their number. Francie, laughing, turned to Adele and realized that her aunt was looking not at the stage, but down at her hands in her lap, her face serious.

"What —" she started to ask, but the Living Nativity began and she turned her attention to the live animals onstage.

When the show ended, Francie sighed. She followed her family outside and discovered that the snow had stopped falling and that the daylight was already fading.

"Rumpelmayer's for ice cream," said her father, "then a quick peek at the tree before we Goldbergs head for home."

At Rumpelmayer's, Francie ordered a sundae. She felt like a princess as she sat at the table with a parfait glass full of strawberry ice cream in front of her. "Only eight days until the first night of Hanukkah," she remarked. "And then Christmas and then New Year's Eve. This has been a great year." She looked around at her family. "Hasn't it?" she added. "But I miss Sadie. I'll be happy to get home and see her."

"Little Miss Chatterbox!" commented her mother.

"But don't you remember feeling excited about the holidays?" asked Francie.

Dana smiled. "Of course I do. And I wasn't making fun of you. I love seeing you so excited." She paused. "I remember one year when your aunt Julia and I were seven, I think, and your uncle Peter was five, our dad suggested that we go to Rockefeller Center to see the tree lit up at night. So we all piled into a cab in the snow — it was snowing just like it was today — and we rode uptown and there was the tree glowing in the darkness. It seemed like magic. After that, we came to Rumpelmayer's." Dana looked around the restaurant. "Doesn't really seem all that long ago. I feel like I could close my eyes now and open them to find Mom and Dad and my brother and sister around the table."

"Were you there?" Francie asked Adele.

Her aunt shook her head. "I was still living in Maine then."

"Well, I'm glad you're here now." Francie rested her head on Adele's shoulder.

"I hate to hurry things along," said Matthew, "but we really should get going. *Someone* has school tomorrow, and" — he turned to Dana — "you and I have an early appointment, remember?"

The Goldbergs and Adele walked back to Rockefeller Center, gazed at the towering tree glowing with thousands of tiny lights, which Francie agreed did seem magical, and at last made their way to Adele's apartment.

"I'm all packed," Francie announced as they walked through her door. "I just need to get my suitcase."

"But before you go," said Adele, and Francie realized with alarm that her aunt's voice was breaking. "Before you go, I —" She sat down heavily on the couch.

"Adele?" said Dana. "What's the matter?"

"I need to talk to you, to all of you. I need to tell you something."

Dana and Matthew exchanged glances, and then they shrugged out of their coats. Matthew dropped into an armchair and Francie plopped into his lap, while Dana sat gingerly next to Adele. She put her hand on Adele's arm. "What's the matter?" she said again.

Adele drew in her breath and let it out slowly. "I've been diagnosed with cancer," she said. "Breast cancer."

Dana's hand flew to her mouth. "Oh."

"I'll be starting treatment in a few weeks," Adele rushed on. "Right after the new year."

"What kind of treatment?" asked Dana.

"Chemotherapy. There may be surgery later. I don't know yet. But they're making great strides in cancer treatment."

Francie buried her face in her father's shirt.

"Hey," said Adele softly. "Listen, we have to think

112

positively. That's the only way to approach this. Square our shoulders and march forward."

"But —" said Francie, raising her head.

"I'll be fine. You'll see."

Dana drew her aunt to her and held her close. After a few moments, Francie realized they were crying. She turned to look at Matthew and saw that he was crying, too. "Is this how we square our shoulders?" she asked.

The adults laughed nervously.

"No," said Adele, reaching for a Kleenex. "No, it isn't. *This* is how we square our shoulders." She straightened up. "Come on. Francie, get your suitcase. It's time for you all to be on your way. No more crying now. I'll see you again in less than two weeks. Christmas in Princeton."

"Not as glamorous as Christmas in New York," said Dana, sniffling, "but it'll do."

"It'll be perfect," said Adele.

"Perfect," echoed Francie. And then she couldn't help herself. She burst into tears and crawled into her aunt's lap, where she stayed until her father drew her gently to her feet.

Chapter 11

Saturday, February 6th, 1982

"Sadie, it's snowing again!" exclaimed Francie. It seemed to have snowed a million times so far that winter — and nearly every snow had fallen on a weekend day or a vacation day so that school had been canceled only twice, to Francie's dismay. Still, snow was snow. And it was even better with Sadie around. "Come on," said Francie. She shrugged into a sweater and ran into the hallway, followed by Sadie.

They hurtled down the stairs to the closet in the front hall and Francie pulled out her mittens, boots, and coat. She was searching for a scarf when her mother called from the kitchen, "Don't you want breakfast?"

"Can I have it later? Please?" Francie called back. "Sadie and I want to play in the snow while it's fresh. Before there are even any footprints in it."

"Okay, but I'm making waffles."

"Really?" Francie paused in her search. Then she looked at Sadie, who was standing on her hind legs at the front door,

114

watching the snow fall. "We'll be back in half an hour, I promise."

When Francie was as bundled up as possible, she opened the door and Sadie bounded into the yard ahead of her. The snow was piled as high as the bottom step of the front porch, and still falling thickly.

"Don't go in the street!" Francie shouted, even though Sadie was struggling through the snow, leaping high but moving forward by inches. Now that she was responsible for another living creature, Francie saw doggie danger everywhere — speeding cars, dognappers (although she wasn't sure what a dognapper looked like), chocolate bars, onions.

She glanced up and down Vandeventer Avenue. Her neighborhood was as quiet as an empty room (and apparently, free of danger). The plows hadn't come down her street yet and she couldn't hear traffic anywhere, not even in town. Across Vandeventer, lights were on in the Newcomers' house, but no one had been outside yet. Next door, she saw footprints in the Foxes' front yard, but they belonged to Hank, who, Francie suspected, had been let out just long enough to pee before he hightailed it back inside his warm, dry home.

Francie bent down to scoop up snow. She packed it into a ball and tossed it to Sadie, who jumped for it and caught it in her mouth, but looked surprised and wounded when it fell apart.

"Let's build a snowman," said Francie. She worked quickly, making three balls and rolling them around the yard until she decided their sizes were right. Sadie leaped up and down at her side. "We'll dress him later," Francie announced when the snowman was completed. "I'm freezing. Let's go get breakfast."

Inside, she found her mother presiding over the waffle iron. "Where's Matthew?" Francie asked.

"Upstairs, working."

"He's been working an awful lot lately," she commented. "He's never here."

Francie ate three waffles before her mother disappeared into her own studio. She turned to Sadie. "You know what this is a good day for? It's a good day for making snowmen and Valentines."

Francie set out paper and markers and glitter and sat at the kitchen table. She had made three cards — one for Kaycee, one for Amy, and one for Fred in Maine — and was wondering whether to make a card for George, when she remembered that Adele's birthday was on Valentine's Day, and decided to make a birthday Valentine for her aunt. She would be able to give the card to her in person, since Adele had said she wanted to spend her birthday in Princeton. The thought made Francie set down the scissors she'd been holding and stare out the window. She wasn't sure she wanted to see Adele next weekend. Adele's hair had already fallen out as a result of her chemo treatments, and during her last phone call to the Goldbergs, she announced that she now wanted to be addressed as Aunt Baldy. Francie had not found that funny in the least. She didn't want a bald aunt.

"Does she have a wig?" she'd asked Dana when they hung up the phone.

"Yes, but I don't think she wears it much."

"She doesn't? Why not?" If Francie were bald, she would wear a wig every moment. She wouldn't want a single person to see her bare scalp. She wouldn't even want to look at it herself.

"She says it itches. And that it makes her look like Betty Boop."

"So she really goes around bald?"

Dana shook her head. "She wears scarves. Her head gets too cold otherwise."

Francie thought about Adele and her bald head under a scarf and she shuddered. Then she turned back to the card.

"Francie? Honey?" said Dana a few minutes later. She poked her head into the kitchen. Francie could see Matthew hovering behind her.

"Yeah?"

"What are you working on?"

"Valentines."

"Could you come into the living room, please? Your father and I need to talk to you."

In that instant, Francie's heart began to pound. She knew, in the inexplicable way you sometimes just know things — like the time she had known moments before it had happened that Matthew was going to fall down the porch steps — that whatever her parents wanted to tell her was going to be very, very bad.

"Okay," said Francie in a small voice, and followed her parents into the living room.

Dana and Matthew sat side by side on the couch and Francie sat facing them in an armchair, Sadie in her lap. "What's wrong?" she asked.

"We have something difficult to tell you," Dana began.

"And we decided to tell you today so that you would have the weekend to start getting used to the idea before you go back to school," her father added.

Francie said nothing.

Her parents looked at each other. At last, Matthew drew in his breath and said, "Your mother and I are going to get a divorce."

Francie stared at them. Then she unearthed Sadie from her lap and jumped to her feet. *"What?"* She sat down again and Sadie slunk from the room. "But — but — you're so happy —" she sputtered. What her father had said made no sense whatsoever.

Dana offered her a sad smile. "Not really, pumpkin."

"I never hear you fight."

"That doesn't have anything to do with it," said Matthew.

"Well, it should."

"We know this comes as a surprise," said Dana. "Let us explain things to you. Please."

Again, Francie said nothing. She crossed her arms.

"We've been seeing a marriage counselor," said Matthew. "We still like each other. We have so much in common —"

"We still *love* each other," Dana interrupted him. "But we're not *in* love with each other. Not anymore."

"So?" said Francie. "You could stay together. Since you love each other and you have so much in common."

Her parents shook their heads. "We've talked and talked about it," Dana continued. "We're just not happy this way."

"What about me?" cried Francie. "Do you think *I'll* be happy if you get a divorce?"

Her mother's eyes filled and she looked down at her hands, which were shaking. "No. Not now. Not at first. But you'll be happy again sometime. And you'll certainly be happier with two parents who are happy than with two parents who are unhappy."

"We want to separate now," Matthew added, "while we're still friendly. We don't want to wait until we're so unhappy that we resent each other and begin to fight."

"You're spending all this time figuring out how to leave each other," said Francie. "Why don't you figure out how to be in love with each other again instead?"

"Pumpkin, trust me; we've been down that road," said Dana. "We've been seeing the counselor for a year."

"Well, obviously he's not very professional," muttered Francie.

"She," said Matthew. "The counselor is a woman. And she's quite professional. We all worked hard to get to this point."

Francie could feel her head start to pound and her chest tighten. She refused to cry, however. "Is it something I did? Is it because of me? What did I do that —" she started to say, and at that moment, an idea occurred to her that was so horrible, she gasped. Her parents must have found out about Erin Mulligan. Maybe they'd somehow found out about everything — about Bubbles and the man in the car and Francie's silence — and they were so ashamed of their daughter that it had torn them apart.

"I can fix it! I'll fix everything," Francie said in a rush, although she had no idea how she could possibly fix what had happened more than two years earlier.

Her parents interrupted her.

"Honey, this has nothing to do with you," said Matthew, just as Dana said, "Oh, Francie, this isn't your fault."

Francie's chest loosened. "But I could still fix it. I know you much better than that counselor does. Why don't you both stop working so hard? Maybe we just need to spend more time together as a family. I'll stay at home more. I won't go over to Kaycee's and Amy's so often. You guys have known each other for years. Why don't you remember the good times —"

Matthew held up his hand. Then he crossed the room and squeezed into the chair with Francie. "I'm afraid this is one thing you can't fix, honey. But we love you even more for wanting to try."

"So," said Francie, feeling her chest tighten again, "what happens next?" She wiggled away from her father.

"Well," said Dana, "we're going to put the house up for sale."

Again, Francie jumped out of the chair, this time causing Matthew to topple over. "You're selling the house? You mean we're moving? *Why?*"

"The counselor feels it will be better for each of us to have a fresh start. And she thinks it's important for you to feel that neither your father nor I left the other, that no one walked out, that this was a mutual decision."

"But why can't you just tell me that and then one of you can keep the house anyway? I don't care which one of you stays, but I don't want to move. I've lived here almost my whole life. I don't remember any other home. Amy is next door, and —"

"We know you love the house and that this is going to be a big change," said Matthew quietly as he and Francie settled into the chair again. "But this is what's going to happen. We've spoken with a real estate agent and the house will go on the market next week. Your mother and I will each look for a new house."

"In Princeton," said Dana.

"Yes, in Princeton. And we hope to find houses that are in walking distance from each other, so that you can go back and forth easily."

"But where will I *live*?" asked Francie, feeling panicky.

"At both places. We'll have to work out a schedule. Maybe divide the week in half — half a week at your mom's, half a week with me. We'll need to think about that. We can make a decision together."

"It won't affect where you go to school," added Dana. "You'll still go to John Witherspoon and then to the high school."

"What about Sadie?" asked Francie, whose voice was now trembling.

Dana sighed. "We can't expect a dog to go back and forth," she said at last. "We've decided that she'll live with me."

"Great. So I'll only get to see her half of every week. This is wonderful. Really wonderful. I couldn't *think* of better news."

"Francie —" Matthew began to say.

Francie got to her feet. "This whole thing is so stupid!" she cried. "Why don't you just stay married? You're only moving about two inches away from each other. Why are you bothering with a divorce?"

"Because we're still friends," Dana replied patiently, "and we'd prefer to keep it that way. We like each other very much. We just don't —"

"I know, I know. You don't love each other. Blah, blah, blah. You know, you aren't the only people in this family. There's one other person — and a dog — to consider." Francie got out of the chair and crossed to the doorway. "Are we done?" she asked. "Can I go to Kaycee's?"

Dana put her hand to her mouth and seemed unable to speak.

"Yes," said Matthew after a moment. "You may go to Kaycee's."

When Francie arrived at the Nobles' house, she took Kaycee by the hand and led her forcefully up the stairs to her room. Then she sat her on the bed and flopped down next to her. "My stupid parents are getting a stupid divorce," she said, and burst into tears.

After her tears had subsided, and after Kaycee had brought her a package of Twinkies and then given her George's guinea pig to hold, Francie told Kaycee everything she could remember about the horrible conversation with her parents.

"Look at the bright side," said Kaycee eventually.

"What bright side?"

"Maybe one of your parents will move onto my street and then we'll be neighbors."

"For *half* the week," said Francie sullenly, although the idea was appealing.

By the end of the afternoon, after eating a second package of Twinkies and after spying on George and his current girlfriend, one of the bra-wearing eighth graders at John Witherspoon, Francie felt slightly better. Dana drove her back to Vandeventer, to the yard with the sad, undressed snowman in it, and the Goldbergs ate dinner together, just as they usually did, as if Dana and Matthew hadn't told Francie that morning that they were going to split the family up and set their daughter's life spinning.

"You seem happier," said Dana as Francie began to clear the table.

"Yes," replied Francie, although she realized that she now carried with her a familiar feeling of dread. But maybe if she tiptoed through these next few months with her parents, maybe if she was as good as she could possibly be, Dana and Matthew would change their minds. Maybe they could still be one happy family, living together in the house on Vandeventer Avenue.

Chapter 12

"Pumpkin?" Dana knocked on Francie's closed bedroom door. "This is the fourth time I've called you this morning. Time to get up. You're going to be late for school."

"I'm *coming*," Francie replied from her bed. "I *told* you."

It was *so* unfair that school started at 8:05.

"Tone of voice!" Dana replied. She opened Francie's door, left it ajar, and returned to the kitchen.

Francie threw back her covers, staggered to her feet, and closed the door, using more force than was necessary. But then she turned and saw Sadie on the bed, lying on her back with her feet in the air, and she ran to her and hugged her. "I can't believe I have to leave you for the whole weekend," she said. "I'm going to be at Matthew's for the next few days. It's Hanukkah, you know. I won't see you until after school on Monday. I'll miss you."

Francie dressed quickly and hurried down the hallway and into the kitchen of the small house Dana had bought

126

after the divorce. She stopped in the doorway when she saw her mother eyeing her.

"Is that what you're wearing?" asked Dana.

Francie looked down at her outfit — jeans and a thin lavender cotton V-neck shirt with three-quarter sleeves. Well, yeah, it was what she was wearing. As in, these were the clothes she had just put on. She rolled her eyes. "Yes. What's wrong with what I'm wearing?"

"It's thirty-four degrees outside. Aren't you going to be cold? Don't you at least want a sweater?"

"Dana. I'll be wearing a coat when I walk to school. And you know how hot it's going to be *in* school. Really. I'm thirteen years old. I think I know how to dress myself."

Dana, her fingers stained with paint, put a piece of toast on a plate and set it on the table. "That's yours," she said. "Eat up. And please, please, let's not let this be the tone of our last conversation before you go to your father's. You stayed up too late last night."

"It wasn't my fault! Mr. Borzak gives us so much homework. And most of it's reading. It takes me twice as long as anyone else to read the assignments."

Dana leaned over and kissed her daughter's head. "And yet you make straight As."

Francie didn't have anything to say to that.

"What are your plans for the afternoon?" asked Dana.

"I'm going to Kaycee's. And then we're going to go to the tree lighting in Palmer Square before I go to Matthew's."

"By yourselves? After dark?"

"Don't worry. George is going with us. And then he and Kaycee will walk me to Matthew's." She paused. "I hope Matthew remembers our plans."

"I'll call him today and remind him."

Francie hesitated for a moment before saying, "Just so you know, what's-her-name might answer the phone."

"Francie . . ."

"I'm sorry. But this is at least his third girlfriend this year. He's as bad as . . . as a thirteen-year-old. I honestly don't remember this one's name. Melanie?"

"Melissa."

"Doesn't it bother you? Plus, he was seeing his very first girlfriend before you guys were even divorced."

"Francie!"

"Well, it's true. He thought he was being so sneaky, but I knew what he was doing."

"We were separated and already living apart, Francie. We were just waiting for the divorce to become official. Anyway, that's not your business. It's ours. Your father's and mine." Dana sat down across from her daughter. "Does it bother you that Matthew is dating?"

Francie shrugged. "It's just weird. Fathers aren't supposed to date. They're supposed to be married." She glanced at Dana and then back at her toast. Her mother had not, as far as Francie knew, been on a single date since the divorce. "Are you going to your studio today?"

"Right after you leave for school."

Dana's house, while perfectly nice, was much smaller than the old house on Vandeventer and didn't have space for a studio. So Dana had rented a small building on Charlton Street, off Nassau. It consisted of exactly one room and a bathroom. Years ago, it had been a tailor's shop. Dana's house, her studio, Matthew's house, and Francie's school were all within walking distance (if you didn't mind a long walk now and then) of one another. Francie had grown used to going back and forth between her two homes, and Sadie had grown used to accompanying Dana to the studio every day. She enjoyed the walk there and back, and while Dana worked, she lay patiently by the door. On warm days, when Dana left the outer door open, Sadie sat at the screen and watched the traffic on Charlton Street.

Dana looked at her watch. "You'd better get a move on," she said.

Francie ran most of the way to school, and by the time she met Kaycee by the main entrance, she was completely out of breath. "Sorry," she said. "It was *so* hard to get out of bed this morning."

"Did you do Borzak's assignment?"

"Just barely. It took me forever."

Francie and Kaycee hustled inside. They were eighth graders now, the same age as the students they had looked up to in awe a mere two years earlier. Amy was a freshman at Princeton High, and George was a sophomore at George School, forty-five minutes away in Pennsylvania. Kaycee would follow him there in the fall, but Francie preferred not to think about that.

The bell rang just as Francie slammed her locker shut. "Yikes!" she exclaimed to her best friend. "See you later."

"I thought today would *never* end," said Kaycee as she and Francie left school that afternoon and started the walk to Kaycee's house. "And I have *so* much weekend homework! It's completely unfair!"

"Tell me about it. I can't believe we have another huge

reading assignment from Borzak. It's going to take me half the weekend to do it. But I'm not starting it until tomorrow. The rest of today is going to be free."

Francie and Kaycee walked through the Nobles' front door just as Mrs. Noble pulled into the driveway.

"It's kind of weird knowing that Mom's at work now while I'm in school," commented Kaycee. "When I was little, it was comforting to think of her at home all day, doing the laundry and stuff. But she must have been bored to death."

The girls waited for Mrs. Noble to lock the car. She hurried along the front walk, laden with book bags.

"What's all that?" asked Francie.

Mrs. Noble smiled. "We started a new unit. Shapes. Today, we worked on big and little triangles. Anybody want to help me go through magazines and cut out photos with obvious shapes in them? I'm going to put up a new bulletin board next week."

"Um," said Francie, who adored Kaycee's mother but really didn't want to work on a preschool bulletin board that afternoon. "Well . . ."

Mrs. Noble smiled at her. "Never mind. You girls go ahead and do whatever you had planned."

"Thanks!" cried Kaycee, and she and Francie ran directly to her bedroom, closed the door, threw off their coats, and flopped on her bed. "Ahh," said Kaycee with a sigh. "Peace. Listen, do you hear that?"

"Hear what?" asked Francie.

"The sound of Borzak not talking."

Francie smiled. "Hey, did you hear about Liam's party?"

"Who's Liam?"

"That guy who wears the top hat."

"He had a party?"

"He's *having* one. Tomorrow night. His parents are going to be away and he invited everyone in our grade."

"Are you *going*?" asked Kaycee.

"Of course not. Matthew and Dana would never allow that. Besides, it's Hanukkah. I'll be at home with Matthew tomorrow night. Maybe you could go, though."

"Are you crazy? I wouldn't be allowed to go either."

"Parents are so unfair."

"Would you really *want* to go to Liam's party?"

"I don't know. No," Francie said. And then wondered why she hadn't said yes.

George hurtled through the Nobles' front door that afternoon just as dark was falling, and stood in the hallway, still wearing his coat. "Kaycee? Francie? Come on!" he shouted.

"Hello, George," said his mother pointedly from the dining room, where she sat at the table, surrounded by open magazines and scraps of paper.

"Hi, Mom. Where are the girls? I'm supposed to take them to the tree lighting."

"Here we come!" called Kaycee.

In minutes, Francie and Kaycee had shrugged back into their coats and were on their way through the quiet streets of Princeton, George between them.

"So, how's everything at John Witherspoon?" asked George. He poked Francie in the shoulder. "Got a boyfriend yet?"

Francie could feel her cheeks flame and was grateful for the darkness. "Nope."

"Francie, he's only teasing," said Kaycee.

"I know." She glanced at George, who towered over her, and then at the sidewalk ahead. Sometimes, it was hard to look at George for too long. It was like staring directly at a perfect sunset.

"Wow," said Kaycee a few moments later. "Palmer Square is mobbed."

Francie was grateful to be distracted. She and Kaycee and George joined in the carol singing and listened to the Princeton High School choir. Then they listened to the shrieks of children as Santa arrived. At last, as Francie watched the dark shape of the tree, it suddenly exploded into thousands of tiny lights. The crowd applauded, and she found herself transported to a Christmas two years earlier, when she had stood on Fifth Avenue in New York City, with Dana and Matthew and Adele, and gazed at the Rockefeller Center tree. Two years earlier, when Dana and Matthew seemed to be happily married and Adele had not yet — not quite yet — divulged her cancer diagnosis.

"Okay, you guys," said George as the crowd started to drift away. "We'd better get Francie to her father's."

Francie was immediately grateful to George for understanding that the house they were walking to did indeed feel like her father's. And her mother's house felt like her mother's. Francie didn't have a "my house" feeling anymore. She had a room at each house, but her family feeling had disappeared in a way she hadn't expected.

George and Kaycee walked Francie to Matthew's and called good-bye to her from the street. Francie waved to them, then approached the front door. She drew in a deep breath, let it out slowly, closed her eyes briefly, knocked, and called, "Matthew? I'm here."

Francie's father enveloped her in a hug. "How's my girl?" he asked.

"Good." Francie smiled. "Is Melan — Is Melissa here?"

"Not yet. She's coming over later. Get settled and then we'll light the candles."

Francie didn't have much to do in order to get settled. She left her backpack full of homework in her bedroom and then joined Matthew in the living room, where the menorah had been set on a table by a window.

Her father was about to strike a match when the phone rang.

"I'll get it!" said Francie. She picked up the phone in the kitchen. "Hello?"

"It's your old aunt Adele," said the voice at the end of the line.

"Adele! How are you?"

"Fit as a fiddle."

This seemed to be true. Earlier in the year, Adele had officially been declared in remission from her cancer. Her hair had grown back, although it was a startlingly different color — nearly orange — her energy was back, and she was hard at work at Bobbie Palombo's. This was so much better than Francie had expected — such good news in a seemingly short period of time (although she was sure it hadn't seemed short to Adele) that she almost couldn't believe it. And yet, whenever she saw her aunt, all she could think was *This is my aunt who had cancer.* The cancer seemed to come first, no matter what Francie tried to tell herself. She had read somewhere that people with cancer shouldn't be defined by their cancer, but this was just what Francie had allowed to happen.

She shook her head.

"I wanted to wish you a happy Hanukkah," said Adele.

"Thank you. We're just about to light the candles."

"I'd better let you go, then. I'll talk to you later."

"Love you," said Francie, and hung up the phone. In the last two years, she had pulled herself away from Adele a bit, just a tiny bit, like paint peeling from a wall. She knew this wasn't fair, but if Adele were to get sick again, Francie felt it would be too much to bear. There had to be some way to make it matter less.

She returned to the living room. "Sorry," she said.

Matthew smiled at her. He handed her a match and Francie lighted the candles, but she had realized recently that the excitement of the holidays seemed to be gone. In two weeks, she and Dana would decorate a tree at Dana's house. Sadie would watch, and Francie would make her wear a red bow on her collar, like she did every year. Dana would laugh and take a picture, and Francie would smile for the camera. On Christmas Eve, four stockings would be hung by the fireplace — Francie's, Dana's, Adele's, and Sadie's. Fun, but not the same.

"I miss Mom," said Francie now.

"Me, too," said Matthew.

Chapter 13

Francie tightened the sash on her bathrobe, tiptoed to her bedroom door, and listened for a moment. She heard only quiet, early morning sounds — a chickadee in the bushes outside her window, the front door opening and closing, probably as her mother retrieved the paper from the stoop. She leaned against the doorjamb and breathed in early morning smells — coffee, the faint scent of shampoo and steam from the shower.

Nothing out of the ordinary.

Cautiously, she opened her door. The hallway was empty, the door to the guest bedroom closed.

"Come on, Sadie," she whispered.

Obediently, Sadie hopped off Francie's bed and followed her down the hall and into the kitchen. Dana was settling herself at the table with a cup of coffee and the paper.

"Anyone else up yet?" asked Francie.

Dana shook her head. "Both still sleeping."

Francie let Sadie out in the yard, then sat down across from her mother. She folded her napkin into a tiny triangle, unfolded it, reached for the container of orange juice, then set it down again.

"Nervous?" asked Dana.

"A little."

"This is going to be a big change for all of us."

"What if Uncle Peter doesn't like it here?"

Dana sighed and shook her head. "I don't know. I'm sure it won't be smooth sailing, at least not in the beginning. But since there really isn't any other choice, we have to make this work."

"I know. But I'm still nervous."

"Me, too."

Francie listened for sounds from the guest room. "I wonder what time Uncle Peter usually wakes up in the morning."

Dana smiled. "I'm sure that's somewhere in the millions of notes Grandma Abby's been making."

"It's kind of weird," said Francie, lowering her voice. "It's like a little kid is moving in with us, but Uncle Peter is thirty-three."

"That's one reason it's getting so hard for your grand-mother to take care of him. It's like caring for a thirty-three-year-old child, and Grandma Abby is in her sixties. It's gotten to be too much for her and Orrin."

Francie nodded. She remembered the evening two months earlier when she'd picked up the phone and heard her grand-mother's voice on the other end. "Hi!" she'd exclaimed, both pleased and surprised. "How are you?"

"I'm fine, honey," Abby had replied, but to Francie, she had sounded tired, on the verge of tears. "Could I speak to your mother, please?"

"Sure," said Francie, who suddenly felt that very bad news was in the air. Her thoughts turned to Adele, and she found Dana in a rush. "It's Grandma Abby," she whispered, holding out the phone. "I think something's wrong."

Francie had sat in the kitchen and listened to her mother's end of the conversation. She was relieved not to hear Adele's name mentioned, at least not at first, but as she'd watched Dana's frowning face, she'd felt a queasiness in her stomach.

"No, of course not," her mother had said. "I understand, but — No, living with Nell is definitely out of the question. She's still in graduate school. . . . Adele offered to take him? Well, that was nice, but I can't see Peter moving to Manhattan." After a long pause, she'd said, "But how do you think Peter will react? Does he know what's happening? He hasn't left Maine in years. Not to mention that he's never lived without you. . . . I know. . . . I know. . . . All right, let's talk again over the weekend."

When Dana had hung up the phone, she'd turned to Francie. "I guess you've figured out that Grandma Abby is wondering if Uncle Peter might come live with us."

"Why?" Francie had wanted to know. "Is — is he hard to take care of?"

"No. Not if you're young. He's a very pleasant man. He's polite, he's friendly, he likes people. He knows how to read and write. He can be funny. But he doesn't know to watch out for danger. You have to help him cross the street. He can't be left alone because he doesn't know how to use the stove and he wouldn't remember to lock the door. He has to be watched and entertained all the time."

Francie had nodded. "But why does he have to move so far away from his home?"

"There really isn't anyone else in the family who can take him. Now that Julia has the twins, she has four kids under the age of five. Nell is still in school. And as for Adele, she isn't *all* that much younger than Grandma Abby."

There had been many more phone calls after that, and, Francie assumed, many conversations between Grandma Abby and Uncle Peter. Yet when they'd arrived the day before, and Peter had bounded out of the car and exclaimed,

"Hi, Francie, my niece! We're here on our trip!" she'd wondered just how much he understood about what was happening.

"Uncle Peter thinks he's just on a trip," Francie said to Dana now.

Dana winced. "Yes. Or at least, that's what he wants to believe. I know Grandma Abby has been preparing him for the move."

Francie heard voices then and whispered to her mother, "They're up."

From down the hall, Grandma Abby was saying, "Today we'll bring the rest of your things in from the car, honey. I'll help you unpack. And then I have to leave. You remember that, don't you? I'm going to leave before lunch."

"And I stay here?"

"Yes, you'll stay here."

Peter entered the kitchen first. "Hi, Dana. Hi, Francie, my niece. This is a nice trip."

Francie saw her grandmother glance at her mother.

"What?" said Dana.

"I didn't say anything," Abby replied.

"You were thinking something."

"Just wondering if you have all the notes I sent."

"Every single one."

"Because you're going to need them."

"I know. That's why I saved them."

"Peter is a big —" Grandma Abby started to say, but when Dana stared pointedly in his direction, Grandma Abby stepped into the dining room. Dana followed her.

"He's a big responsibility," Francie heard her grandmother continue.

"Well, this was your idea. If you think I'm such an unreliable member of this family, why did you entrust me with him?"

"I don't think you're unreliable —"

"I've raised a daughter, you know."

Francie looked from Peter, who was standing uncertainly in the kitchen, to her mother, whose face, she could see, was turning red. "Um, Mom?" she said. "Grandma Abby?" She inclined her head toward Peter, and her mother and grandmother returned to the kitchen.

Peter sat heavily at the table. "Is this my place?" he asked. "Are we having pancakes for breakfast? I like pancakes."

"You do?!" said Dana in an unusually bright voice.

At that moment, Francie heard the sound of scratching at the back door, followed by an annoyed woof from Sadie. "I forgot she was outside!" Francie cried. She rushed for the door and returned to the kitchen, Sadie at her heels.

Peter leaped up from the table and retreated to the hallway.

"She won't hurt you," said Francie. "Remember? Remember last night? She just wants to be your friend."

"I don't want a dog friend."

"Francie, put Sadie in your room," said Grandma Abby.

"What?" Francie cried. "That's not fair. She —"

"Mother," said Dana. "I think we know how —"

But Francie headed off the argument. "Okay, okay."

She led Sadie down the hall to the bedroom and closed the door quietly, saying, "It's just for a little while. I promise. You're a good girl. You didn't do anything wrong."

When she returned to the kitchen, she leaned against the counter and watched Peter eat his breakfast. Dana, who had been unprepared to make pancakes, had served him toaster waffles. Peter was cutting them up sloppily and chewing with his mouth open. But he was enthusiastic with his praise. "These are *good*, Dana! These are very good." A piece of waffle fell out of his mouth and landed on the floor. He leaned over, picked it up, and put it back in his mouth. Francie squeezed her eyes shut.

Across the table from Peter, a conversation was taking place that he seemed unaware of.

"You have the list of foods he won't eat," Grandma Abby was saying, leafing sternly through a sheaf of papers that were covered with her handwriting. "The list changes frequently, but these are the ones he won't eat now. And there's no point in trying to force him to eat anything he says he doesn't want. It's just not worth the trouble. Everything else you need to know is here, too — bedtime, morning routine, TV shows. Oh, and this is somewhere in the notes, too, but it's critical — he absolutely never remembers to look before he crosses the street. You have to hold his hand —"

"I know. You've told me. Listen, my main concern," said Dana, interrupting her mother, "is the day-care situation. I sent you the brochure for the place I found. He'll only need to go there when I'm at the studio, but that will probably be four days a week."

"He should be fine. He used to go to day care sometimes at home."

"I like day care," said Peter suddenly.

Dana brightened. "Great! We'll visit the new place tomorrow."

"The new place?"

"The one you'll be going to here in Princeton."

"I don't want to go to day care in Princeton."

"Honey, you'll have to go there when I'm at work and Francie is at school," said Dana patiently.

Peter looked helplessly at Grandma Abby. "Will you go with me?"

His mother shook her head. "No. I'm leaving before lunch today, remember?"

Francie made a mental note not to say, "Remember?" to Peter all the time.

Francie steeled herself for a horrible, heart-wrenching good-bye scene in the front yard that morning, but when Grandma Abby's suitcase had been loaded into her car, and she and Dana and Francie were standing nervously on the lawn with Peter, he said, sounding very adult, "Drive carefully, Mom."

Grandma Abby looked at Dana and Francie in surprise. Then she laughed and said, "I will. And I'll call you tomorrow night." She wrapped her arms around Peter and embraced him for a long time. "I love you."

"Love you, too."

Francie hugged her grandmother, and then Dana and Abby stood, facing each other.

"Thank you for this," said Abby stiffly. "I don't know what Orrin and I would have done if —"

Dana waved her off. "I wanted to do it. Peter is my brother. You know how I feel about him. Anyway, this is what families are for. Isn't it? Sometimes we have to say good-bye in order to move ahead."

Grandma Abby stepped away. She nodded quickly, gave Peter another hug, climbed into the car, and backed down the driveway.

"Wait!" cried Peter, but his mother was pulling onto the street. He turned to Dana. "When is she coming back?"

"You'll see her over the summer, but this is your home now."

"No!"

Francie took her uncle's hand. "Hey, Uncle Peter," she said, "did you know there's a secret garden behind our house?"

"What? A true secret garden?"

Francie nodded. "I'll show you. And also, the kid next door? His name is Richie, and he can make armpit farts."

Peter laughed. "Francie, my niece, you are not supposed to say *fart*!" He glanced at Dana. "But it's funny."

"Yes," agreed Dana, who was smiling. "It is funny."

"Dana, I'm going to take Uncle Peter on a private tour now."

"A private tour . . ." Peter repeated, sounding awed.

Francie led her uncle toward the house. "It starts inside. I'll give you the special private tour of our house and then a tour of the neighborhood."

"Will I see the secret garden and kid who makes the armpit . . ." Peter's voice trailed off, but then he said gamely, "the armpit farts?"

"If he's at home. Come on." Francie opened the door for Peter. "Now, the first thing to know about our house," she began, "is that Sadie could turn up almost anywhere. She especially likes my bedroom, but she also likes the kitchen, the laundry room, the couch in the living room, and the window seat in the dining room. She could turn up anywhere. She's kind of like an Easter egg."

Peter raised his eyebrows. "Wow."

"So the tour will start now, and while we're looking around, you try to find Sadie, okay?"

"Okay," Peter replied solemnly.

The tour lasted ten minutes, and Peter located Sadie on a pile of towels in the laundry room.

"You found her!" exclaimed Francie.

"Yes." Peter backed away, but said nothing. And when Francie announced that Sadie was going to join them on the tour of the neighborhood, he didn't object.

Peter took in the secret garden, which was a narrow strip of yard between the side of the house and a toolshed, where Dana and Francie had set out a birdbath, several bird feeders, and a small statue, and planted a row of rosebushes, now just beginning to turn a bright spring green. They turned onto the street and Francie suddenly grabbed Peter's hand. If he couldn't be trusted to cross the road by himself, then he certainly wouldn't know not to get into a car with a strange man to take a peek at a puppy named Bubbles.

Francie held tight to Peter while he studied the homes along the street and the small brook two blocks away. Her uncle was disappointed when no one answered the bell at Richie's house, but was greatly pleased that afternoon when first Kaycee and then Amy dropped by to meet him.

Bedtime did not go as smoothly as the rest of the day.

"That isn't my bed," Peter announced as he stood in the doorway of what had been the guest room but was now filled with his things.

"I know it's all new," said Dana, "but this is your room and that's your bed."

Peter shook his head. His eyes filled with tears. "Can I call Mom?"

"I'm sorry, honey," said Dana, "but she isn't home yet.

She won't be home until tomorrow. You'll have to wait until then. She'll call you as soon as she can."

"But I need her!"

"You have us," said Francie, peeking into the room. "Let's all read together. You get in bed, I'll sit in the chair over there and read aloud, and Dana will sit on the floor with Sadie. Look at all the picture books we have. We'll each choose one. Except for Sadie, since she can't talk." Peter smiled. "You choose first," Francie continued.

"I choose *Peter the Important*. You wrote that, right, Dana? You wrote it about me?"

"I wrote it about you and I wrote it *for* you."

"Because I'm your brother."

Peter climbed into bed and lay flat on his back, his arms folded behind his head. He was asleep before Francie had reached the end of the story.

Chapter 14

Wednesday, June 20th, 1984

"Good morning, Francie! Good morning, Francie, my niece," Peter exclaimed in his husky voice. "Today is your big day." He lumbered into the living room, where Francie was assembling her outfit for the afternoon. "Graduation day," he added. "Where's your cap and gown?"

Francie smiled at him. "Unfortunately, we don't get caps and gowns. It's just eighth-grade graduation. So this is what I'll be wearing." She pointed to the black skirt and white blouse she had laid on the back of a chair. "The boys wear black pants and white shirts."

"No caps?" Peter asked.

Francie shook her head. "Sorry. But there will be singing. The graduates — all the eighth graders — are going to stand on risers and sing songs we've been learning in chorus."

When Peter continued to look disappointed, Francie added, "We get diplomas, though. Rolled up and tied with gold and blue ribbons. Gold and blue are our school colors."

"Well," said Peter after a moment. "Okay."

Sadie wandered into the living room, sniffed at Francie's outfit, then crossed the room and sat at Peter's feet. He reached down to stroke her head. "What do *I* wear to your graduation, Francie?" he asked.

By now Francie knew her uncle well enough to realize that what he was really asking was whether her graduation was an opportunity for him to wear his good suit, which he adored.

"Ever since my brother was a little boy," Dana said once to Francie, "he has loved getting dressed up."

"You get to wear your suit," Francie told Peter now. "*And* Dana and I bought you a new tie to go with it."

"Really? A new tie? Thank you, thank you!"

Peter threw his arms around Francie and gave her a bear hug.

Francie smiled again. She was trying very hard to be excited about her graduation, but she had a feeling she wasn't nearly as excited about it as Peter was. She knew that the graduation should mark the beginning of new adventures, of the next step in her education, blah, blah, blah. But all Francie could see were ends of things. The end of middle school, the separation from Kaycee, who would soon follow her brother to school in Pennsylvania. Sure, Francie would join Amy at Princeton High, but Amy would be a year ahead of her, and Francie would start off in the fall as a lowly freshman without her best friend at her side. It was not appealing.

"But you know we're still going to be best friends," Kaycee kept saying. "We're best friends for always. We'll still see each other after school —"

"You won't get home until almost five every day."

"Then we'll see each other on weekends."

"It won't be the same. These are the kinds of things parents tell you when they're getting divorced. 'Just think of all the one-on-one time we'll have.' 'We'll still be able to see each other half of each week.' But it really isn't the same, and everyone knows it."

Kaycee had sighed. "I don't know what to tell you. I still feel like we'll be best friends our whole lives. Think about it: Even if I were going to go to Princeton High with you, eventually, we'd go to different colleges. Did you think our friendship would end then?"

"No," Francie had muttered.

Now she looked at her uncle, at his open, happy face, and she smiled. "I'd better get going. I'll see you at the ceremony this afternoon."

The John Witherspoon Middle School graduation was to be held at two o'clock that afternoon. At one thirty, the eighth-grade girls were directed to the girls' locker room and the boys were directed to the boys' locker room. They changed into their black-and-white outfits, and shortly before two, they lined up in the gym. The weather had "cooperated" (as Matthew would say), and the ceremony was to be held outdoors. The bleachers for the students had been set up facing rows of metal folding chairs for the guests.

"Can you believe this day is here?" Kaycee whispered to Francie as they jostled to line up alphabetically.

"I really can't," Francie replied, once again feeling a sense of melancholy wash over her.

"Places, students!" called the vice principal. "Right now!"

Francie and Kaycee hugged briefly, then rushed to their spots in the line. Francie could hear the school band tuning up, and as the graduates finally filed out the door and toward the bleachers, the band began playing "Pomp and Circumstance."

Francie gazed straight ahead (at the back of Robin Glover's neck) until she had reached her spot on the bleachers. Then she turned and faced the audience. At first, all she could see was row after row of heads glistening in the June sunshine. How would she ever locate her family? She held up her hand to shield her eyes from the glare and suddenly she caught sight of an arm waving wildly. "Francie, my niece!" called an excited voice.

Peter, of course. He was half standing, resplendent in his suit and his new tie. Dana tugged him back into his chair, and that was when Francie realized that seated all together in a row were her mother, Peter, Adele, Matthew, and Matthew's latest girlfriend, Maura. Melissa/Melanie was a thing of the past. She had been followed by Valerie, then Kim, and now Maura. Francie detected something different in Matthew's relationship with Maura, though. It was steadier. It had started more slowly. And Matthew had taken greater care when he'd introduced Francie to Maura. Francie thought Maura might one day become her stepmother, although Matthew had said no such thing.

How could Dana stand it? Francie wondered. There she was, sitting four seats away from the woman her ex-husband was probably going to marry, with no spouse of her own on the horizon. Yet she looked perfectly calm. Dana had not dated one single solitary guy since the divorce. She had thrown herself into her painting and her writing, and then into providing a home for Peter. She never said a word about being lonely or about wanting a husband, and she seemed content enough to spend time occasionally with Matthew and Maura.

"I don't get it," Francie had said more than once to Kaycee. "I just don't get it."

"Does she seem happy?" Kaycee had wanted to know.

"Well, yes."

Kaycee had shrugged. "Then I guess she's okay with the way things are."

Francie had let the subject drop.

Graduation officially began when Junette Shavers blew a note on her oboe and the band played the first bar of "You Are the Sunshine of My Life." After two stanzas, the graduates joined in the song, swaying from side to side in time with the music. Francie saw Peter swaying in the audience, bumping shoulders alternately with Dana and Adele, who smiled indulgently at him. For some reason, this sight made her tear up and, for several moments, she was unable to sing. Robin Glover glanced curiously at her, but Francie stared straight ahead, willing her tears to dry up and her throat to open up.

After two more songs, the principal, Ms. Danow, walked to a microphone that had been placed before the risers. She welcomed the guests, saying, "Thank you all for coming to honor the John Witherspoon class of nineteen eighty-four as they reflect on their years here and set out on the path to their futures with open minds and open arms."

In the audience, Peter stealthily pulled a package of M&M's out of his pocket. Dana noticed this immediately, took the package from him, and dropped it into her purse.

"We will now," Ms. Danow continued, "announce the winners of our eighth-grade awards. Award recipients will be presented their plaques along with their diplomas. We'll start with our scholastic achievements. The John Barr Award for excellence in science goes to Genetha Gray. The Hamilton Palmer Mathematics Award goes to Kendall LaPlaca. . . ."

Francie grew so interested in watching Peter, who apparently had hidden a second bag of M&M's in his pocket and was now surreptitiously eating the candies, that she almost missed hearing Ms. Danow say, "And finally, the John Witherspoon Award for excellence in written composition goes to Frances Goldberg."

Francie jumped at the sound of her name and grinned when her family leaped to their feet and began applauding, Peter scattering M&M's as he did so.

Half an hour later, the ceremony was over and the graduates, shirts untucked, ribboned diplomas stuffed into their pockets, streamed off the bleachers and onto the lawn, where they joined their families.

"Francie!" Kaycee called. "Over here!"

Francie, who hadn't yet located her parents in the shouting, jostling crowd, turned in the direction of Kaycee's voice. They ran into each other's arms.

"We did it!" cried Francie.

Kaycee pointed to the plaque Francie was clutching. "Way to go! Excellence in composition. You're going to be a writer someday, just like your mom."

"And my grandfather," said Francie.

"Girls! Look this way!"

Francie and Kaycee turned around to find Kaycee's father aiming his camera at them. They grinned. Then they grinned for Matthew's camera, for Dana's camera, for Mrs. Noble's camera, for Adele's camera, and finally, for Peter's old Instamatic.

When the picture taking ended, Kaycee pulled Francie aside and whispered urgently, "Guess what! We just got invited to a party."

"A party? What party?"

"Tonight. At Junette's house. Everyone is going. It's a *boy-girl* party."

"Are you sure *we're* invited?" asked Francie.

"It's like I said. Everyone is invited. Junette's going up to anyone and saying they can come. It's sort of spur-of-the-moment."

Adele put her arms around Francie and Kaycee. "What's all the whispering, girls?"

"We got invited to a party!" exclaimed Francie. "A

boy-girl party. Do you mind if I go, Adele? I know you're only spending one night with us." She didn't wait for an answer. "Dana," she said. "Come here." She tugged her mother away from Matthew and Maura. "Junette's having a party tonight and she's inviting everyone. Can I go? Please?"

"Who's Junette?" asked Dana. "Where are her parents? I need to talk to them."

"Mom! You can't do that! That's so embarrassing." Francie looked helplessly at Kaycee, who was saying to her own parents, "It's the first time Junette's ever invited us to anything. Please, can we go?"

"If we talk to her parents first," said Mr. Noble. "We have to make sure they'll be on hand tonight."

"Dad, no!" cried Kaycee.

"Honey, all we need to do is talk to them."

"Absolutely," agreed Dana.

"We're not babies," said Francie and Kaycee.

"Exactly. You're *teenagers*," said Kaycee's mother. "We need to know that there won't be any drinking or —"

"Mom!" cried Kaycee again.

"I'm sorry. No party unless we talk to the parents," said Dana.

"Oh, *man*," said Francie. "Then I guess I'll just stay home tonight. Thank you for ruining my life."

Francie's anger dwindled as the day went on. It was hard to stay angry during a pizza celebration at Conte's with the Nobles and later at home as she was presented with gifts from her parents and Adele and Peter.

"Do you like it? It's a journal," said Peter as Francie tore the paper off a gift that her uncle had apparently wrapped himself. "I bought it with my own money."

"It's wonderful," said Francie. "Thank you." She hugged her uncle.

It was later, after Peter had gone to bed and Matthew and Maura had left, that Adele suddenly seemed to droop on the living room couch.

"Tired?" Dana asked her. "It was a long day."

Francie flopped onto the couch beside her aunt. "I'm tired, too," she admitted, and then leaned over to whisper to Adele, "Don't tell anyone, but I'm glad I didn't go to Junette's party after all."

Adele gave her a half smile.

"Are you *sure* you're okay?" said Dana, settling herself on the arm of the couch.

Adele didn't answer, so Dana, frowning, said, "Francie, put on the water for tea."

Francie left the living room but returned as fast as she

could, just in time to hear Adele say, ". . . wasn't going to tell you right away, but the cancer is back. I got the test results the day before yesterday. There's a spot on my lung and several spots on my bones."

Dana sagged against Adele. "Oh no."

"The doctors say there are lots of things they can try," Adele went on. "More chemo. But nothing they can operate on."

Dana leaned forward, head bowed. "No," she said. "I thought you were out of the woods. I thought this was over. It can't be."

Adele pressed her fingers to her lips and said nothing further.

After a moment, Dana put her arms around her aunt and rocked her back and forth.

Francie pressed her fingers against her eyes.

Finally, Adele forced a smile. "No more surgery," she said shakily. "At least I won't have to go under the knife again."

Francie couldn't speak. She sat down on the couch, and she and her mother hugged Adele from both sides. "I love you," she said into Adele's shoulder.

Chapter 15

Tuesday, January 15th, 1985

"Francie? Are you sad today?" asked Peter.

"Yes. I'm very sad. I've been sad for a long time."

"Me, too."

"I know," said Francie. "And it's okay to be sad. We're all sad."

"I don't like feeling sad."

"Well, no. I don't either. I'm just saying it's okay to feel that way."

"How long will we?"

"How long will we what? Feel sad?"

Peter nodded and Francie shrugged.

"Will we feel better after the funeral?" Peter persisted.

"Maybe. A little." Francie was growing tired of his questions. "Uncle Peter," she said, "why don't I start breakfast while you feed Sadie? Matthew will be up soon —"

Peter, who had been sitting patiently at the kitchen table, even though it wasn't set and he had been the only one awake in the house, suddenly leaped to his feet and exclaimed, "Everything is different!"

"I know," said Francie. "I know it is." She put her arms around her uncle and whispered, "I'm sorry. But it won't last forever, I promise."

Peter pulled away from her. "When is Dana coming back?"

"In a few days. But you'll see her today."

"At the funeral?"

"Yes."

"Okay," said Peter, who, instead of feeling comforted, suddenly burst into tears. Which was all it took for Francie to burst into tears as well.

"Oh dear," said a voice from the doorway.

Francie turned to see Matthew, still in his pajamas, tufts of hair sticking up stiffly. He'd been sleeping in Dana's room for several weeks, ever since Dana, on a visit to New York, had called Francie to say, "Adele's going back into the hospital and I think I need to stay here for a while."

"How long is a while?" Francie had wanted to know.

"I'm not sure, pumpkin. Several weeks, maybe."

What Francie had wanted to say was "Several *weeks*? Why are you staying for several weeks? Adele must be really sick this time." But she hadn't wanted to jinx things by speaking those words. So what she'd said instead was "Several *weeks*?

But what about Uncle Peter? I can go to Matthew's, but Uncle Peter's never stayed there before."

"I'm going to call your father next," Dana had replied. "I'll see if he can move in with you and Peter."

That had been the beginning of the long, slow weeks during which, Peter complained, nothing was the same. Dana stayed in Manhattan, living in Adele's apartment, and spent her days at the hospital with Adele. Matthew moved into Dana's house to take care of Francie and Peter and Sadie. Sometimes, Maura stayed with them; sometimes, she stayed at her own place. Francie slogged through her days at Princeton High, days that were as lonely as she had feared they would be. She'd worked hard that fall, and she liked her teachers, but she missed Kaycee and found that her energy was focused on Adele, not on making new friends. She got up, went to school, came home, and closed herself into her room with her homework. She phoned Adele frequently, and on weekends, if Adele wasn't in the hospital, she and Dana and Peter drove into New York to visit her. Sometimes, Grandma Abby and Orrin would visit then, too; sometimes, Aunt Rose and Uncle Harry. Once, to Francie's surprise, Papa Luther and Helen had been at Adele's apartment, both of them standing formally in front of the window, while Adele rested on the daybed, looking as though she wished they would leave. Then, when they finally began to say their good-byes, Adele had burst into tears and clung to Papa Luther, who had patted her back awkwardly.

At last, there came the Saturday in December when Dana had visited on her own, leaving Peter in the care of Francie and Kaycee. It was late that afternoon when she'd called to say she needed to stay in New York. Matthew moved into Dana's house, and after that, the weeks had rolled out torturously slowly until there was another phone call from Dana, this one placed from the hospital. "She's gone," Dana had said.

Francie had handed the phone wordlessly to Matthew, crept to her room, and sobbed into her pillow.

Three days later, it was time for Adele's funeral.

"*I want —*" Peter started to say vehemently, but Francie interrupted him.

"Uncle Peter's going to feed Sadie now," she told her father. "And I said I would start breakfast. When are we leaving for New York?"

"In an hour and a half," replied Matthew. He hugged first Francie, then Peter, and added, "I know this is a hard day, but let's get on with things. We have a lot to do, and we don't want to be late."

"But we're sad," said Peter.

"We're all very sad," Matthew agreed, "but you know what Adele would say."

"What?" asked Peter.

"She would tell us to buck up."

"Or she'd make a joke," added Francie.

"I can't think of any jokes," said Peter. "Not today."

Francie turned and began rummaging in the refrigerator. She couldn't prop Peter up any longer. She had run out of energy.

Adele's funeral was held in a church not far from her apartment. She had never attended the church — she hadn't attended any church since she'd moved to Manhattan — but Bobbie Palombo, who helped Dana arrange the service, pointed out how much Adele had liked her neighborhood. "I think she'd want us all together in this place she loved, don't you?" she'd said.

Dana later told Francie she thought that what Adele would *really* have wanted was a rousing funeral held in a Broadway theatre, with an orchestra and costumes and an audience sing-along, but Dana had agreed to the church, grateful for Bobbie's help.

"We aren't going to the funeral in Maine, are we?" Francie asked Matthew as they wound their way through

Adele's west side neighborhood, looking for a parking spot near the church. "I love Maine and Grandma Abby and all, but I don't feel like seeing Papa Luther again. I mean . . ."

Matthew held up his hand. "Say no more. I know exactly what you mean. And Adele would know, too. That's why she wanted two separate services."

Matthew found a spot at last, and he and Francie and Peter stepped out of the car and walked toward the church, sloshing through graying snow and avoiding icy patches, Peter crying, "Don't let me fall!" every few steps.

When Francie saw her mother, she left Peter with Matthew and ran into Dana's arms. "I hope you have Kleenex with you," said Francie at last, pulling back from Dana, "because I forgot mine."

Dana wiped away tears, hers and Francie's, and opened her pocketbook. "I stuffed almost a whole boxful in here," she said shakily.

Francie looked at the wads of Kleenex and tried to smile. "I don't see anything in there *but* Kleenex."

"Where is she?" asked Peter, shuffling up to Dana and Francie, on Matthew's arm.

"Who?" asked Dana.

"Adele," said Peter, frowning, as if Dana had forgotten something as basic as what the cow says.

"Adele?"

"I want to see what a dead person looks like."

Dana burst into tears again, and Matthew took Peter aside to say that there would be no casket at the service and that no one would be seeing any dead bodies. "She's going to be buried in Maine," he said.

Inside the church, Francie and her family met with Bobbie Palombo in a private room. "We want you to sit with us," Dana told Bobbie. "You've been like family to Adele."

Bobbie's face, which Adele had once said looked as if it were made of granite, crumbled and her lips quivered. "And I know what you meant to Adele," she replied. "You were like her daughter." She rummaged in her own purse, which turned out to hold as much Kleenex as Dana's did.

Francie looked at Dana with a start. Dana had lost her mother, she realized. She supposed it didn't matter how old you were when your mother, or the person you considered your mother, died. When that connection was severed, you were suddenly — whether you were prepared or not — let loose in the world, on your very own at last. Francie thought Dana looked terrified.

The priest of the little church stepped into the room and looked at Dana. "It's time," she said. "Everybody ready?"

Dana nodded. "I'll go first, then you, Francie. After that, Peter, then Matthew, then Bobbie. We'll sit in the first pew."

Francie had expected to see a scattering of people in the seats behind the first pew. When she followed her mother and the priest into the front of the church, she was so surprised by the crowd that had gathered that she faltered, missing a step, and Peter bumped into her from behind.

"Dana!" Francie whispered loudly. Every pew was filled, and more people stood at the back of the church, and even up and down the side aisles.

Dana reached for Francie's hand as they slid into their pew. "Adele had a lot of friends," she whispered back.

The service began. The organist played "Sheep May Safely Graze" by Bach, followed by Gershwin's *Rhapsody in Blue*.

Dana subtly withdrew several tissues from her purse and handed one to Francie.

Bobbie, granite face once again in place, walked to the front of the church and spoke about Adele, recalling the day she'd applied for her job at the costume shop nearly thirty years earlier and told Bobbie she had no experience in the costume-making business whatsoever. Francie smiled, expecting a joke, but all Bobbie said was that Adele had assured her that if she hired her, she wouldn't regret it.

"And of course I didn't," said Bobbie. "She turned out to be one of my most talented designers."

Francie heard sniffles behind her. Then Peter started to sob loudly and the sniffling in the church increased. Bobbie waited for a moment, began to say something else, hesitated, held a tissue to her eyes, and retreated to the pew.

The service continued. Later, when Kaycee asked Francie about the funeral, Francie was able to give her only the vaguest information. She couldn't remember specifically what Bobbie had said, couldn't remember what had happened after Bobbie sat down. Her memories involved Kleenex, leaving the church, and later arriving at Adele's old apartment with Dana, Matthew, and Peter.

"Now you come home with us?" Peter said hopefully to Dana as they shed their coats and stood in the tiny living room.

"No, honey. Remember? I have to stay here to clean out the apartment. But I'll be home in a few days. Probably by the weekend."

Peter flopped onto the couch and pouted.

"Could I stay with you?" Francie asked Dana. "Please? I could help you go through everything. We'd get it done twice as fast."

"That's a nice offer, but you already missed school yesterday and today. You'd better go back with Matthew and

Peter." Dana drew Francie aside and whispered to her, "Peter will be lost without you, honey. He's not ready to be separated from both of us. He needs you."

Francie sat next to Peter on the couch and looked around at Adele's things — the birdcage that had never held a bird, the lamp with the beaded shade. She looked at the pink and blue walls, at the bed and dresser that had belonged to Dana when she'd left her family in Maine and moved in with Adele.

"What are you going to do with everything?" she asked her mother.

Dana shrugged and pursed her lips. She couldn't speak.

"Can I have something of Adele's?"

"Of course," Dana said. "Of course you can. Anything you want. Peter, you, too. Take a look around and see what you want."

Peter asked for the lamp shade (just the shade), even though he didn't have a standing lamp in his room.

"I don't know what I want," said Francie. And then her eyes fell on a row of photo albums on the bottom shelf of Adele's bookcase. She sat on the floor and paged through them while her parents talked about plans for the next few days. Francie looked at pictures of Adele in front of theatres with people she didn't recognize, and pictures of Adele on vacation with people she didn't recognize. Then she found an album of photos of Adele with Dana and her family when Dana was a little girl, and finally, an album of photos from the 1940s and even earlier. She realized it was the album Adele had brought to Thanksgiving dinner the year before they'd found Fred. She wondered if anyone had told Fred that Adele had died, and whether he would even remember her.

"Can I have the albums?" Francie asked.

"Absolutely," Dana replied. "I wouldn't have given them away."

"Can I take them with me now?"

"Sure."

When darkness had fallen and Matthew said it was high time they hit the road, Dana walked down to the street with Francie and Peter and Matthew, helping them juggle the lamp shade and two cartons containing the albums.

"See you Saturday," Francie called as her father pulled their car into the traffic on the crowded side street.

Dana waved to her and turned away, once again wiping her eyes. Francie fumbled for the box of tissues her mother had given her.

Peter said fiercely, "Don't anybody talk to me right now."

Chapter 16

Wednesday, April 30th, 1986

"Francie?" Dana called from the living room. "Matthew just pulled up."

"Coming!" Francie stood in front of her mirror and examined her outfit. She wasn't sure what to wear to the PHS award ceremony. Nobody would be very dressed up, but she wanted to look nice anyway. Nice, but not dressy. She longed for the days when she and Kaycee used to spend every afternoon together. Kaycee would have known exactly what Francie should wear.

She reminded herself that she had other friends now. It had taken forever (she seemed to be a late bloomer), but she had at last made new friends. She could phone Isabel. Or Beth. Or Dale.

"Francie!" Dana called again.

"Okay!" Francie took one last look at her outfit — new tight-fitting jeans over a pair of short black boots, which had used up a good chunk of her babysitting earnings; a long, loose blue-and-purple-striped sweater; a chunky purple bracelet that Peter had given her for Christmas; and a pair of gold hoop earrings that had belonged to Adele.

She burst out of her room, calling, "I'll be back before nine. Matthew said he'll pick me up at eight thirty, when the ceremony is over. See you later!"

"Bye, honey," said Dana vaguely. She was seated at the kitchen table, reading through the page proofs of her newest book.

"Bye!" called Peter, who was watching an old episode of *Bonanza* on the VCR. Francie noticed that he was wearing his ancient holster and cowboy hat, prized relics from his childhood.

She hurried through the front door and out into the cool evening air. "Hi," she said to Matthew as she climbed into the front seat of his car. "Thank you for driving me. Dana's working tonight."

"No problem. What time did you say I should pick you up?"

"It's supposed to be over at eight thirty. It starts at seven thirty. But you never know. It might run a little over."

"No problem," said Matthew again.

Francie studied her father's hands on the steering wheel, her eyes drawn to his left hand, where she knew he would soon be wearing a wedding band.

"What?" asked Matthew, glancing at her.

Francie smiled. "Nothing. Just thinking about the wedding."

Matthew smiled back at her. "Are you sure you're okay with it?"

"I'm sure," she replied quickly, although what else *could* she say? No matter what she thought of Maura, she couldn't exactly say to her father, "You know, I really don't think you should marry her. She's nice and all, but I'd rather not have a stepmother." Luckily, she didn't need to say any such thing. She liked Maura very much, and knew that Maura and her father were happy together.

"You'll get to be a junior bridesmaid," Matthew pointed out, and that thought truly did make Francie happy. She'd tried on her dress and felt she looked rather glamorous in it. Amy Fox had said she looked like Adele's lamp shade, but for once, Francie had disagreed — and said so.

As Matthew approached Princeton High, Francie could see that the school was lit up. A line of cars was snaking toward the parking lot.

"I'd forgotten what a big deal this is," said Francie.

She barely remembered the previous year's ceremony, when she'd been a freshman. Adele's funeral had taken place just three months earlier, and afterward, Francie felt as if she'd steered through her life from within the confines of a cocoon. Somehow, she had managed to navigate each school day, focus on her work, and bring home excellent grades. Period. She saw no friends except Kaycee and Amy on the weekends. She joined no clubs. She wrote no stories. Dana's life seemed to have halted as well. Her writing had come to a stop. She focused on Francie and Peter, and on cleaning the house. Francie had never seen such a clean house.

Then the warm weather had arrived and Francie had discovered that she was beginning to shed the cocoon. She found the journal Peter had given her for her eighth-grade graduation and wrote down random thoughts and phrases that she thought might work themselves into a story. At the same time, Dana began sketches for a new picture book. Francie accepted a summer babysitting job for Richie and his armpit-farting brothers next door. Dana hired a cleaning service. Francie spent weekend afternoons at the community pool with Kaycee and Amy and some of Amy's friends, including Isabel, Beth, and Dale, who were in Francie's grade and had soon become her friends, too. By the time September had rolled around and her sophomore year of high school had begun, Francie felt free of the cocoon. She still thought of Adele every single day, and knew Dana did, too, but more often she remembered things that made her laugh rather than cry.

"There are Beth and Dale!" Francie said to Matthew now. "You can just drop me off here. I'll wait for you on Moore Street later, not in the parking lot, okay?"

"Okay. Have fun."

Matthew drove off and Francie ran to her friends.

"Come on, you guys," said Beth. "Hurry up so we can get good seats. I don't want to get stuck in the back."

They joined a crowd of kids from all classes who were streaming into the building.

"Why do you care if we sit up front?" Francie asked Beth as they squeezed through the back doors.

"Because then we can look into the balcony and see whose parents are up there."

"What?"

"Don't you remember last year?"

Francie didn't mention her cocoon. "No, not really."

"The winners of the awards are kept secret. From the students anyway. But the parents are notified ahead of time and they're given seats in the balcony so they can be here to see their kids receive their awards."

"Oh," said Francie. "I guess I'm not getting an award, then. My father just dropped me off. And Mom's working tonight."

They reached the auditorium and Dale said, "Plenty of seats up front. Come on."

They settled into three seats in the fourth row, saving another seat for Isabel. Francie read her program. Beth swiveled around to check out the balcony so often that Dale said her neck was going to unwind and blast off.

Presently, Isabel arrived, flopped into the empty seat, and elbowed Francie in the ribs. "Look, there's Joel," she whispered.

Francie did not immediately look at the spot to which Isabel was pointing. Joel Morris was one of the most popular boys in the sophomore class — and one of the nicest.

"Put your hand down," Francie hissed. "He'll see you pointing."

Isabel grinned.

Two seconds later, Beth let out a shriek. "Francie, your parents and Peter are here!"

"What? No, they're not. They can't be."

"They are, too. Look."

Francie craned her neck around and saw, in the very first row of the balcony, Dana, Peter, Matthew, and Maura. They grinned at her.

Francie grinned back. "How did they even do that?" she

asked her friends as she faced front again. "My mother was at home working, and my dad said —"

"What does it matter?" Dale interrupted her. "They tricked you! Now you know you're going to get an award."

Francie tried to quell the butterflies that were dancing in her stomach. The lights dimmed in the audience and were turned up on the stage, the room grew quiet, and then something happened to Francie that hadn't happened in a while.

Her memory flicked to a black station wagon and a handsome man with a puppy named Bubbles. Francie closed her eyes briefly and sank low in her seat. She thought about Erin Mulligan. She thought about Erin Mulligan's parents. If Erin were alive, she would be a freshman at PHS and this would be her parents' first opportunity to sneak into the balcony and cheer for their daughter as she won an award for sports or citizenship or math. Francie turned around, glanced at her family again, then faced forward and tried to focus on the members of the PHS band as they tuned up their instruments. Was every happy moment going to be like this? she wondered. Would she mark every milestone with thoughts of Erin, with the absence of Erin? And how many years — how many, many years — would have to pass before the sight of a black station wagon no longer sent a trail of fear down her back or made her immediately check to see that Peter was safe?

Was this the price Francie paid for keeping her secret?

Francie won the sophomore creative writing award. She walked onto the stage and accepted it from the principal with trembling hands. From the balcony, she heard Matthew let out a whistle and Peter shout, "Yay, Francie, my niece!" Her thoughts were a blur of Erin Mulligan and Adele, of Mrs. Pownell and her parents and her grandfather Zander Burley, the famous writer.

An hour later, the ceremony ended. The lights were turned up in the audience, and Francie edged down the row of seats, clutching her rolled-up certificate, following Isabel and Beth and Dale. She was making her way toward the back of the auditorium, wondering how to find Dana and Matthew, when she felt a hand on her shoulder and she turned around.

"Hey."

Francie blinked. Joel Morris was grinning at her.

"Congratulations," he said.

Francie indicated Joel's own certificate. "Congratulations to you, too."

"I was wondering if you'd like to go to Conte's with me."

"What? Right now?"

"My mother can drive us."

Francie's butterflies returned, thumping madly in her stomach. "Let me just check with my parents. I'll meet you by the front doors."

"Francie!" squeaked Dale, the moment Joel was out of earshot. "You have a date! With Joel!"

"You're living out my dream," Isabel whispered frantically.

Ten minutes later, permission having been granted for a quick slice of pizza with Joel, Francie found herself sitting in the backseat of Mrs. Morris's Chevette, trying to focus on something other than the heat that was being generated by the left side of Joel's body.

"Francie, your mother is going to pick you up in an hour, is that right?" asked Mrs. Morris as she pulled the car up in front of Conte's.

"Yup. Um, thanks for driving us."

Francie followed Joel out of the car, hoping any number of things: that she wouldn't spill while they were eating, that she wouldn't say something stupid, that her bra wouldn't somehow unfasten itself during the meal and spring apart. And none of those things did happen. What Francie couldn't recall later when first Isabel, then Dale, and finally Beth called to ask her for details about the date, was what *had* happened.

Except for one thing. As she and Joel had left Conte's on their way to meet their parents, who were already waiting for them, Joel had leaned over, quick as a cat, and kissed Francie lightly on the lips.

"Good night," he had whispered. "See you tomorrow."

"Night," Francie had replied.

She slid into Dana's car and touched her fingertips to her tingling lips.

Chapter 17

Saturday, February 14th, 1987

Francie woke slowly, letting the sounds and smells of a February morning in Maine seep into her foggy brain. She lay still, eyes shut, feeling Dana's presence beside her in the bed, in the little room at the top of the house in Lewisport. At last, she opened her eyes, rolled over, sat up, and peered outside, across Blue Harbor Lane at the roiling ocean. The day was dreary, and the sky and sea were leaden gray. Francie stared at the horizon, having difficulty telling where the sea ended and the sky began. Then she shifted her attention to the beach and watched the waves pound the rocks on the shore, sending plumes of spray in showers above the sand.

It was the perfect dismal day for a funeral.

Francie shivered, found a sweatshirt, and pulled it on over her nightgown. She added a pair of wool socks and began to tiptoe downstairs. Before she reached the second step, she heard Dana shift position, and she looked over her shoulder to see that her mother had sprawled out and taken command of the entire bed.

Francie reached the bottom step, still shivering, and made a beeline for the thermostat, which she edged up several degrees. She turned around and found Peter standing behind her, and she jumped.

"Did I scare you?" asked Peter.

"No," Francie lied. She knew Peter hadn't meant to scare her. "I just didn't realize you were up yet. Are you hungry?"

"Yeah."

"Let's start breakfast, then."

Peter followed Francie into the kitchen and sat at the table while she pulled eggs and bread and juice from the refrigerator.

"I miss Sadie," he announced.

"I know. I miss her, too. But she couldn't come with us on the train. I'll bet she's having fun with Matthew and Maura."

"Yeah."

"Are you ready for today?"

"Yeah."

"Really? Do you remember what's going to happen?"

"Yeah."

"What?"

"We're going to Papa Luther's funeral."

"That's right."

"Francie," said Peter after a moment, "I don't feel as sad as I did when Adele died."

Francie glanced at her uncle. "Neither do I. I think that's because we knew Adele a lot better than we knew Papa Luther." And, she thought, because Papa Luther never entirely accepted either one of us.

"Yeah."

"Today's Adele's birthday, you know."

Peter shot Francie a look of surprise.

"I mean, it would have been her birthday. It's Valentine's Day. Adele would have turned fifty-two today."

"Francie? How did Papa Luther die?"

Francie hesitated. Papa Luther had been eighty-nine years old. He'd died in his sleep, peacefully, at the end of a perfectly normal day. But Francie didn't want Peter worrying about unexpectedly dying in *his* sleep. "He was very old," she said cautiously.

"It was his time to go?" suggested Peter.

"Yes, I guess so."

"Will I wear my suit today?"

"Yes."

"Okay."

Another church, another funeral. While Adele's funeral in Manhattan had been attended almost solely by friends, Luther's was attended by a smattering of friends, and by dozens and dozens of members of his big extended Maine family. Francie stepped cautiously out of her aunt Julia's car and stood on the soggy lawn in front of the church in Barnegat Point. It was the same church, she knew, in which Papa Luther had married Helen, his second wife, the wife who wasn't a whole lot older than Grandma Abby, her stepdaughter.

Francie looked at the relatives who were hurrying into the church, sidestepping puddles and wrestling with umbrellas as they ran along the walk toward the oak doors. She watched Peter catch sight of Grandma Abby and Orrin, and lumber in their direction, calling, "Hi, Mom! Hi, Dad! Look at my suit!"

Francie saw Aunt Rose and Uncle Harry. She saw Rose and Harry's grown kids and their families. She saw Nell, Dana's younger sister. Climbing out of the car behind Francie were Aunt Julia, Uncle Keith, and their children. Francie thought of Fred, who wouldn't be attending the service, but whom she and Peter and Dana had visited the day before. Fred had lost his father, Francie realized, although she didn't think he quite understood that.

Francie scanned the crowd for Helen and saw her entering the church on the arm of a man Francie thought might be her son Miles.

"It feels a little funny to be here," Francie said to Dana, whispering again.

"Pumpkin, you really don't have to whisper."

"This time I do. It feels funny to be here," she went on, "because of what Papa Luther thought of me. And because of what I thought of him *because* of what he thought of me. I feel . . . what's the word? I feel *hypocritical.* All I wanted from him was for him to accept me as I am. But I thought less of him, because of what he thought of me. So. I was hypocritical, too."

"I suspect you aren't the only one here who feels hypocritical," Dana replied with a wry smile.

Francie shook her head. "Wow. I hope the people who go to my funeral someday won't be whispering and feeling like this."

"I think that's one worry you can cross off your list." Dana held out her hand to Francie. "Come on. Are you ready to go inside and get this over with?"

"I guess. Boy," Francie grumbled, "Matthew really lucked out. Papa Luther hated him so much, he didn't even have to come to the funeral."

"Papa Luther didn't hate Matthew," Dana said, frowning.

"Didn't he?"

"*Hate* is a pretty strong word."

"Papa Luther had a lot of strong thoughts."

"But I don't think he hated your father. I think he just disapproved of him."

"Well, that's even worse! Hate says something about the person who's doing the hating, about the hater himself. But being disapproved of — that says something about *you*, the disapproved-of one. That you're, I don't know, *wrong*, somehow. Disapproval is so quiet and behind the scenes. You can't fight it. And it makes you feel really bad about whoever you are."

Dana had taken Francie by the arm and, elbows linked, they'd begun to make their way among the puddles to the door of the church. Now she pulled Francie aside and they stood under the dripping eaves.

"What?" said Francie nervously.

"Is that the way you think Papa Luther felt about you? That he disapproved of you?"

"Yes," said Francie. "Sure. Dad and Uncle Peter, too. Papa Luther disapproved of us, so he never accepted us. Me and Matthew because we're Jewish, and Uncle Peter because he has Down syndrome. Even Fred, his own son! He might just as well have come out and said, 'I think I'm better than all of you.' "

Dana stared across the lawn at the cars lining the road and beyond at the houses of Barnegat Point, the businesses at the west end of the main street, the roof of the high school. She turned back to Francie and blinked. Then she said quietly, "If you don't want to go inside, you don't have to. I would understand, and I don't care what anybody else thinks. There isn't time to find someone to run you back to the cottage now, but you could take the umbrella and go to the coffee shop. We could pick you up later. Do you want to skip the funeral?"

Francie shook her head. "No. It's okay. Papa Luther was still my great-grandfather. If it weren't for him, I wouldn't be here." She smiled.

"Francie, my love, you are far more mature than I'll ever be," said Dana, and at last, they entered the church.

By the time the funeral for Luther Nichols, father of Abby, Rose, Fred, Miles, and the late Adele; husband of Helen and also of the late Nell; owner and founder of Nichols Furniture; resident of Barnegat Point since 1932 — by the time his funeral had come to an end with one final wheezy note from the organ, the sun had come out.

Francie emerged from the church into a bright, chilly afternoon that glistened in the morning's raindrops. She squinted her eyes.

"Dana!" Peter exclaimed, hurrying from Abby's side. "Now we go back to the cottage? Now we go to the beach?"

"No, honey," Dana replied. "Sorry. It's too cold for the beach, and anyway, we have to go to Helen's for a while."

Francie watched her uncle's face fall. "We have to go to *Helen's*?" he repeated.

Dana nodded. "There's a reception. We have to pay our respects to her. We have to show her that we love her and support her. She feels very sad right now."

Peter scowled. "I already said I'm sorry."

"I know you did, but we have to go anyway."

Peter was still complaining when Aunt Julia squeezed her car into a spot on Haddon Road across from Helen's house and Francie climbed out of the backseat, where she'd been sitting with her cousin Finn crammed onto her lap.

"How long do we have to stay?" muttered Peter as they approached the house. "I hate this place."

Dana took his hand but didn't reply.

Francie said nothing until they'd been ushered inside by a maid who, Francie felt, was probably older than Luther had been. Then she took a look around at the crowd of black-frocked guests and whispered to Peter, "It's like a flock of crows landed in here."

Peter laughed.

Francie felt a hand at the small of her back and turned around. "Julia's going to take us back to the cottage in two hours," Dana told her. "Can you last for two hours?"

"Sure." Francie was privately pleased to be in the company of her mother's family. So many cousins and aunts and uncles. She was happy to be surrounded by them. Helen and, possibly, Miles were the only ones in the house who cared the least bit about whether anyone was Jewish or had Down syndrome, and Francie steered clear of the two of them. She had organized several of the youngest cousins into a quiet game of telephone, when, from across the room, she heard Grandma Abby say, "Do you want to spend tonight with Dad and me, Peter? Before you go back to New Jersey?"

Peter, who had been sitting restlessly in a chair near the front door, leaped to his feet. "Yes! Yes, that would be great! Dana! Mom said I can spend the night with her."

Dana looked sharply at her mother. "You said what?" she exclaimed.

The game of telephone ground to a halt and Francie rose to her feet.

"I asked him if he wanted to spend tonight with Orrin and me before you leave," said Abby.

Dana let out a loud sigh. "It would have been nice if we'd talked about this earlier. Now someone will have to go back to the cottage and collect his things. And Julia will have to pick him up at your place tomorrow before she picks up Francie and me. She'll have to get up at the crack of dawn."

Abby let out a sigh of her own. "May I remind you that Peter is my son?"

"Well, of course. All I'm saying is that we should have planned this ahead of time. There are other people to consider here. Not just you."

"And not just you."

"Meaning?" said Dana.

"The world doesn't center around Dana Burley."

"The world doesn't center around anyone."

"Dana?" said Francie, stepping forward.

Her mother held up a hand and Francie retreated.

"Don't you *ever* take my feelings into consideration? All I want is a night with my son," said Abby.

"What about a night with me? I'm your daughter."

"Where was this attitude when you were fourteen and went off to live with Adele?" asked Abby.

"I don't know. I was *fourteen*."

"Come on," said Francie, stepping forward again. "Don't fight. Please. Not here. Not in front of Peter. And everyone else." She glanced at the row of children, who were paying close attention to every word.

But Dana and Abby held their angry gazes until finally, Dana said, "Julia, I'm sorry to make you do this, but Mom has just invited Peter to spend the night with her, so we'll have to go back to the cottage for his things. Do you mind running me to Lewisport?"

"What, now?" said Julia.

"Nice, very nice," muttered Abby.

Francie, powerless, slipped out of the house and sat on the porch steps alone.

Chapter 18

Thursday, June 16th, 1988

"Frances Adele Goldberg." The voice intoned Francie's name as if a period followed each word: Frances. Adele. Goldberg.

Francie, heart pounding, stood at the head of a line of students on the lawn of Princeton High School. The principal, Mrs. Allen, who was poised next to a podium, hand extended and clutching a rolled-up diploma, appeared to Francie to be miles away. She was, in fact, twenty feet away.

Francie felt frozen. Her blue gown rippled in a warm breeze, and from the corner of her eye, she could glimpse the fluttering tassel on her cap, but her limbs seemed disconnected from her brain and wouldn't move. Just when she feared her name would have to be called a second time, Harrison Goldman, standing behind her, nudged her shoulder, and Francie stumbled forward. She reached Mrs. Allen, and the vice principal, who was manning the microphone, now added, "With high honors," and a cheer rose from the crowd of parents and guests seated on the lawn.

Francie finally relaxed. She held her diploma aloft and, grinning, filed back to her seat, joining the brand-new members of Princeton High School class of 1988. She flopped down next to Carla Glassman.

"We did it!" said Carla. "It's over."

That was not at all how Francie felt, but she didn't know Carla well enough to contradict her. High school might have been over, but the rest of her life was just beginning, a sentiment that had been reflected in every speech given that afternoon — by Mrs. Allen, by the class valedictorian, and by the class president.

The rest of her life.

The rest of her *life*.

Francie was awed by the phrase. What felt like an entire life was already behind her, and yet the rest of it, which she hoped would be much, much longer, still lay ahead.

"How does it feel to graduate?" Peter had asked her that morning. He had been excited about Francie's graduation from middle school, but he was fascinated by her graduation from PHS — and the thought that she would soon leave Princeton and go to college.

"Well," she'd replied, "it feels . . . grown-up. It feels like I've reached a milestone."

"You *have* reached a milestone," said Dana, who was sitting in the living room with Francie, Peter, and Sadie. "In a couple of months, you'll be on your own."

"I don't know if I'm ready for that."

"Of course you are," said Dana.

"I wish I could be on my own," said Peter.

Francie had smiled at him. "You need to stay here and keep Dana company while I'm at college. And you have to help her take care of Sadie."

"That's a big job," said Peter solemnly.

"If you had to name the top ten highlights of the last four years," Dana said to Francie, "what would they be?"

"Mo-om!" Francie rolled her eyes. "That sounds like an essay question on a college application."

But Peter had leaned forward in his chair. "What *would* they be?"

Francie had let out a breath. She leaned over to pat Sadie, who leaped neatly into her lap, turned around twice, and curled herself into a comma. "The last four years," Francie had repeated. "Well, graduation, of course, even though it won't happen for a few more hours. Graduation is certainly a highlight. Do I have to list these in order or can I just name ten things?"

"No order," said Dana. "And they don't have to be ten good things either. But ten important things."

"All right, then. Matthew's wedding and being a bridesmaid."

"I got to be an usher and wear a tux!" exclaimed Peter.

"You were the best usher there," said Dana.

"Number three," Francie continued, "Matthew and Maura's baby. Sorry if these things are about Matthew, Dana, but they are important. I have a baby brother now. Let's see. Okay, number four, well, Adele's funeral, of course."

"Don't talk about that," said Peter, so Francie said hastily, "Number five, Curtis."

"Woo-woo! Francie has a boyfriend!" Peter hooted.

Francie refrained from adding that Curtis was her steady boyfriend, the only boy she'd dated for the past year, and the boy she would continue to see over the summer — and after she'd left for Smith College, although she wasn't sure how that would work, since she would be in Massachusetts and Curtis would be attending the University of Colorado. But Curtis insisted that they could make it work.

"Six?" prompted Dana.

"Getting accepted at Smith."

"You got accepted everywhere you applied."

"I know, but Smith was my first choice." Francie shifted Sadie in her lap. "Number seven, learning to drive. Number eight, the trip to the Grand Canyon with Kaycee's family. Number nine, winning the writing award last week."

"Your third writing award," Dana pointed out.

"Number ten?" said Peter.

Francie screwed up her face. Then she smiled. "This," she said.

"What?" asked Dana and Peter.

"This moment right now. All of us here together, Sadie in my lap."

"We do this all the time," said Peter, frowning.

"And I'm really going to miss it after I leave. What am I going to do without you when I'm at Smith?"

"You'll find friends," said her mother. "You won't believe how fast you'll find friends. And they'll become your family."

"Maybe I don't want a new family."

"But you won't lose your old one. As you get older —" Dana started to say.

Francie and Peter looked at each other and groaned. "Not something else about getting old!" cried Francie.

"I didn't say, getting *old*, I said, getting old*er*. As you get old*er*, you'll find that you have lots of families. And they'll all be important to you, but in different ways. You'll have us, and you'll have a family of childhood friends, and you'll have a family of new friends. At Smith, you'll sit around with these new friends — and by the way, I promise that some of these friends will become your very best friends, friends you'll keep for the rest of your life, no matter where you live — anyway, you'll sit with these friends and you'll talk and laugh and cry and share all sorts of things. It might be hard to imagine now, but let's have this conversation again in six months. I have a feeling things will look pretty different. Maybe you won't even want to be sitting here with your old mother."

"You mean, my old*er* mother," said Francie. "And please don't start crying, Dana, or else *I'll* start, and then Uncle Peter will start, and then we'll spend graduation day having a cry fest."

When the graduation ceremony was over, when the PHS class of 1988 was mingling noisily with parents and brothers and sisters and friends under a clear sky on a sticky June afternoon, Francie saw Curtis signal to her, and she broke away from Kaycee and Amy. Her oldest friends had been in the audience that afternoon, sitting with Dana, Peter, Matthew, Maura, and eighteen-month-old Jordan. Amy had finished her freshman year at Denison University and was back in Princeton for the summer. Kaycee had graduated from George School two weeks earlier, and Francie had attended the ceremony, cheering for her friend as she received her diploma.

"Back in a minute," she said now as Curtis waved to her from the edge of the lawn. She made her way through the crowd to Curtis, who kissed her quickly and said, "What are you doing now?"

"Going back home. To Dana's house, I mean. She and Matthew planned a family party, remember?"

"I know, but skip it," said Curtis. "Come with me."

"Skip it? I can't. The party is for *me*. I'll see you tonight at your house."

"There's going to be a huge crowd, though."

Francie wanted to say, "Whose fault is that?" but she kept her mouth shut.

"We won't have any alone time," Curtis went on.

Francie frowned. "We have the whole summer. We'll make plenty of alone time. I promise."

"Why do you have to spend so much time with your family?"

"Because they're my *family*."

Curtis sighed. "All right. Come early tonight, though, okay?"

"I'll try. I'm driving Beth and Dale —"

"Beth and Dale will be with you? So we can't even grab a few minutes at the beginning of the party?"

Francie closed her eyes briefly. She loved Curtis, but he seemed to require an awful lot of her time. And patience. "I'll see what I can do," she said vaguely.

Dana and Peter had made a banner that read CON-GRATULATIONS, GRADUATE! and hung it over the garage doors. Francie burst into tears when they pulled up to the house after the graduation festivities and she saw it for the first time.

"What's wrong?" asked Peter. And then, in alarm, he added, "Did we make a spelling mistake?" He turned to study the sign.

Francie wiped at her tears as she and her mother and Peter climbed out of the car. "No, it's perfect!" she said. "Thank you. I'm happy, not sad. Really."

All afternoon, she kept bursting into tears. She burst into tears when Matthew and Maura arrived for the party and Maura handed Jordan to her. She burst into tears when her parents gave her a box that contained a gold ring with her birthstone embedded in it. She burst into tears when Peter donned his cowboy hat for the party, and later, at the mere sight of Sadie. Finally, Dana said to her, "Pumpkin? Do you need a little time to collect yourself?"

"I guess so. I think I'll go to my room for a while before I leave for Curtis's. Is that okay?"

"Of course."

Francie sat on her bed, Kleenex in hand. She looked around her room and wondered which of her possessions she would take with her to Smith. She thought about Erin Mulligan, who should have been completing her junior year at PHS. She thought about her grandmothers, Grandma Abby and Nonnie, neither of whom had had the chance to go to college. She examined the photos stuck around the edges of her mirror: Francie and Kaycee and Amy, waving sparklers in the dark on a long-ago Fourth of July evening; Sadie as a puppy, guiltily edging out of the kitchen with a pilfered bagel in her mouth; Adele with a thoroughly bald head; Matthew and Dana, much younger, seated formally on a couch; Jordan when he was two hours old.

She knew she had a photo of Curtis somewhere but she couldn't find it.

Francie sat and thought and finally dried her eyes and rejoined her family.

Chapter 19

Tuesday, August 30th, 1988

"Are you sure you're okay with this?" Dana asked Peter as he hesitated by the Nobles' car.

Peter touched the brim of his cowboy hat. "Yeah."

"It's just for one day, remember?"

"Yeah."

"And you'll have Sadie for company. I'll be back in Princeton late tonight and I'll pick you two up on the way home. Okay?"

"Okay." Peter peered inside Dana's car, which was packed for the trip to Northampton, Massachusetts. "I really can't come with you?"

"Sorry, honey. There's barely enough room for Matthew and Francie and me."

"Plus," said Mr. Noble from inside his own car, "we have a big day planned. You're going to join us on a Noble family picnic."

This, Francie knew, was what Kaycee and George had requested before *they* went off to *their* colleges, and they'd planned the picnic to coincide with Peter's visit — the very first time he'd spend an entire day away from his family.

"Okay," said Peter again. Reluctantly, he opened the back door of the Nobles' car so that Sadie could jump in.

"Wait!" cried Francie. "What about my good-byes?"

For a moment, just for a moment, Peter turned his head away, and Francie thought he was going to stomp angrily into the car and leave in silence. Then he turned back to her, opened his arms, and wrapped her in one of his bear hugs.

"Good-bye, Francie, my niece."

"Good-bye, Peter, my favorite uncle. I'll write to you every week, I promise. And we can talk on the phone, too. And you're going to visit me on parents' weekend."

"Even though I'm not a parent?" asked Peter, pulling back to look Francie in the eye.

"Even though you're not a parent. But I'll see you long before then. I'll be home for October break. Now let me say good-bye to Sadie."

Sadie, who had turned around mid-jump, was now sitting patiently on the ground by Peter's feet.

Francie bent down and took Sadie's face in her hands.

Sadie raised her eyebrows one at a time and stretched her mouth into a smile. "Good-bye, old girl," Francie whispered.

Peter helped Sadie into the car then, walked around to the passenger side, and climbed in beside Kaycee's father. They drove off and Francie burst into tears.

"Oh no! Don't start that now!" wailed Dana. "We'll be crying all day."

Francie was relieved that she had said good-bye to Kaycee, Amy, Beth, Isabel, and Dale the day before. Then, that evening, she had also said good-bye to Curtis. They had sat squished together in the front seat of his car, parked several blocks from Dana's house on an isolated stretch of road.

"We'll talk every day we're apart," Curtis had said. "Every single day."

Francie had felt anxious rather than reassured. "*Every* day? You know, that might not be possible. I have a feeling we're going to be awfully busy."

"Too busy for a phone call? There's always time for a phone call."

"But I won't have a phone in my room," said Francie. "I'm going to be sharing one with three other people. I think we'll keep it out in the hall. It won't exactly be private."

Curtis appeared not to have heard her. "And you can come visit me on your fall break."

"What? No, I can't! How am I going to pay for a plane ticket to Colorado?"

"Then I'll come visit you."

Francie felt smothered, as she sometimes did at the end of a long snowy winter when she'd been confined to her house too often.

"Let's see how it goes," she had muttered.

Curtis had frowned at her, but then he'd softened, taken her face in his hands, and kissed her.

"Seriously," Dana said now. "Let's save our tears for the moment Matthew and I are ready to leave Northampton this afternoon."

Francie made a huge effort and largely succeeded. Dry-eyed, she crammed herself into the one teensy spot that Matthew had cleared for her in the overpacked car. Dry-eyed, she watched, first her street, then Nassau Street and the university pass by as they made their way to Route 1. By the time they were flying along I-95, she had fallen asleep. But she awoke feeling jittery and apprehensive when Matthew called from the front seat, "Almost there!"

Francie closed her eyes again. *I'm not ready for this,* she thought. *I am so not ready.*

She leaned forward. "Maybe I could take a deferment," she said suddenly. "Maybe we should leave and come back next year."

"And what do you propose to do between now and then?" asked Dana just as Matthew said, "Look! There's a sign for Smith College."

Francie slumped back into her seat. "I don't know."

Matthew, following directions that Dana read from a pad in her lap, turned off the highway and onto a road leading into Northampton. He made a left on Main Street, and before Francie knew it, she saw Grécourt Gate, and beyond it, the brick buildings of Smith College.

Dana directed them to the dorms on the Quadrangle, and Francie, now a bundle of nervous energy, looked around her in awe. The roads were jammed with packed station wagons and anxious parents looking for parking spots.

"Hey!" exclaimed Matthew as he finally pulled into the Quad. "What do you know? A spot right in front of the door to Gardiner House."

Francie looked up at the ivy-covered dorm that would be her home for the next four years. "Let's turn around right now," she whispered.

Neither of her parents answered her. Matthew had already slid out of his seat and was opening the back of the station wagon. "What floor are you on?" he asked.

"Fourth," muttered Francie.

"The *top* floor? I hope there's an elevator."

There wasn't. Francie and her parents struggled up three flights of stairs, lugging as many items as they could carry. When they reached the double room Francie would be sharing with a girl named Claudia Werner, they discovered that the Werners must already have arrived. One of the single beds was neatly made, one of the closets was full of clothes, and several cartons were stacked in a corner.

"She's tidy," Dana commented approvingly.

"But this room is . . . sterile!" exclaimed Francie. It was true. Except for Claudia's things, the room held only two beds, two dressers, and two desks. A yellowing shade hung at each window.

"Once you two have unpacked, it will look better," Matthew promised.

Francie and her parents made several more trips up and down the stairs before the car was emptied. Francie's side of the room was now a colossal mess. "Will you guys stay for a while and help me with this?" she asked.

"Is that a stalling tactic?" replied Dana.

"What we should really do," said Matthew, "is go into town and get a bite to eat. Then we'll open a checking account for you at Pioneer Bank, and after that, your mother and I should be on our way."

Francie flopped on the bed and groaned.

"What's wrong?" said a voice from the doorway.

Francie sat up. A tall girl with long dark hair smiled at her. "Francie?" she said.

"Claudia?"

"Yup. What's wrong?"

"Well . . . I don't know."

"We're just about to go into town," Dana said. She held out her hand. "I'm Dana, Francie's mother."

"And I'm Matthew," said her father. "Would you like to have lunch with us?"

"Have your parents already left?" asked Francie before Claudia could answer. Her roommate seemed awfully calm.

"They're saying good-bye to my sister. She's a senior. She's in Cushing House."

"So you've been to Smith before?" said Francie.

"Tons of times. You're going to like it here. I promise."

"And I promise I'm not always this messy. I just need to put everything away."

"Do you want to go shopping later?" asked Claudia. "This room needs some plants. And some character."

Dana grinned. "Character. Definitely."

"Francie, I hate to say this, but we really should get going," said Matthew. "Claudia, would you like to come with us?"

"I would, but my parents are coming back to say good-bye. I'll wait for you here, Francie, okay? Then we can do something about this room."

Years later, after Francie and Claudia became graduates, after they became mothers, after they became grandmothers — years later, they would remember this meeting. They would remember deciding to go shopping so that their room would have character. They would remember the trip that afternoon to the store on Green Street, where they would buy mugs and posters and two pothos plants that they named Irene and Henrietta. Irene and Henrietta would live long lives. After graduation, Irene would move back to Princeton with Francie, and Henrietta would move to Houston, Texas, with Claudia, who by then would already be married. The daughter she would have one day would be Francie's goddaughter.

Francie hurried her parents through lunch at a restaurant called Fitzwilly's and later through their business at the bank.

When her checking account had been opened and a book of checks was safely stowed in her purse, she returned to Gardiner House with her parents. The tearful good-bye she had feared turned into a rushed good-bye as other freshmen kept peeking through the open doorway to Francie and Claudia's room and introducing themselves.

"Let's all sit together in the dining room tonight," said one.

"Meeting in the Smoker after dinner," said another.

"Hey, are boys allowed in —" another started to say, and then noticed Dana and Matthew.

"I think it's time for us to leave," said Matthew. Francie didn't disagree.

"I'll walk downstairs with you," said Claudia, "and then we can go shopping. Oh, and I want to show you Paradise Pond. . . ."

Francie paused just long enough by her parents' car to give Matthew and Dana each a quick hug. "I'll call you Sunday," she said. "We can have Sunday morning phone calls, okay?" She and Claudia waved to the car as it circled the Quad and exited through the archway. Then they put their arms around each other and made their way to Green Street.

"How is it possible," said Claudia later that afternoon, "to know that someone you've just met is destined to become your lifelong friend?"

"I don't know, but it is. You know, Dana told me this would happen — that I would find a family of friends here at Smith — and she was right." She paused, then added, "She's always right."

Francie ate her first Gardiner House meal in the dining room that night at a table of other freshmen, Claudia at her side.

"The food is pretty good," she said.

"For the most part," said Claudia. "Just wait until liver night."

"Maybe I'll become a vegetarian."

"Me, too."

"Vegetarians can eat chocolate, right?"

"In my world, they can," said Claudia.

"Hey," said the girl sitting across from Francie (Francie thought her name was Sue), addressing the entire table. "You know the house meeting tonight in the Smoker? We're supposed to go in our nightgowns."

"Seriously?" Francie replied, immediately feeling uncomfortable. She turned to Claudia. "I can't go in my nightgown!" she whispered desperately.

"If you don't, you'll be out of place."

"Are you going to wear yours?"

"Yes. You know what happens at the end of the nightgown meetings in the Smoker? We get to eat Dunkin' Donuts that the seniors buy."

"I do like donuts," said Francie.

That evening, Francie and Claudia gamely attended their first house meeting wearing their nightgowns. They ate donuts and eyed the seniors, who seemed eons older than the freshmen. Later, they fell into their beds. Just when Francie was starting to feel tearful, imagining her mother and Matthew and Peter and Sadie at their homes in Princeton, she heard Claudia say from across the room, "Good night, Irene. Good night, Henrietta."

Francie began to laugh. Then she and Claudia, lights out, talked until Francie's clock read 2:46.

Epilogue

Friday, July 15th, 1994

Francie stood on Vandeventer Avenue in Princeton, gazing up at the old Victorian house. "Those were my bedroom windows," she said, pointing to the second floor. She gripped her husband's hand. "Boy, did I spend a lot of time looking out of them. I used to stare at the Newcomers' house and wish I had brothers and sisters." She laughed. "All those Newcomer children."

She had watched for the black station wagon, too, obsessively peering down at the street in the days following her encounter with the man and Bubbles. But this she kept to herself.

George Noble looked over his shoulder at the house across the street. "Do the Newcomers still live there?" he asked.

Francie shook her head. "They moved away when I was in high school."

"So what do you think?" asked George, turning back to Francie's old house.

"What do I *think*? Are you serious? It's my dream to live here again. I *loved* this house. But can we really afford to buy it?"

George frowned. "I think so. I mean, you know as well as I do. We've done the math."

Francie nodded, recalling the nights she and George had sat in their apartment outside of Princeton, hunched over their bank statements and a pad of yellow paper, figuring, then figuring again.

Francie had graduated from Smith just two years earlier. On a sunny day in May, she had said tearful (very tearful) good-byes to Claudia and Sue, to friends she had known since her first day at Smith, and to friends she had met during her senior year. They had hugged and hugged and hugged some more. They had exchanged addresses. They had promised to keep in touch forever, to come back for every reunion, to name their babies after one another. Finally, Dana had looked pointedly at her watch and Matthew had opened the car doors. Five minutes later, Francie and her parents were once again driving around the Quad. Then they were inching through Northampton, and soon enough, they were flying down I-95. Francie suddenly felt as though the last four years had been a mirage.

They already seemed as unreal as they had before she had lived them.

Francie had spent her first summer as a college graduate as Matthew and Maura's live-in babysitter, taking care of Jordan and his little sister, Sarah, who had been born during Francie's sophomore year at Smith. She and Claudia had written lengthy letters to each other — sometimes ten or more pages long. On the days when Matthew and Maura hadn't required her services, she took the bus to New York City to interview for jobs in publishing, and to visit Dana, who had moved there not long after Peter died.

Francie remembered in great detail the phone call she'd received at the beginning of her junior year, a year she'd been dreading, since most of her friends, including Claudia, had decided to take their junior year abroad. She'd been sitting cross-legged on her bed late one lonely, rainy Saturday night, looking out the window of her room in Gardiner House — a single that she cherished, although she still missed Claudia's company — when her phone (her very own phone!) rang.

"Hello?" she'd said, automatically checking her watch and trying to figure out what time it was in Europe.

"Hi, honey," said Dana.

Something in her voice made Francie's breath catch. "What's wrong?" she'd asked.

"It's Peter."

"Peter?" Francie had been expecting to hear that Sadie — aged, deaf, arthritic Sadie — had died. She and Dana had been talking about this and trying to prepare Peter for what surely lay ahead.

"He's in the hospital. He caught a cold; it turned into pneumonia and . . ." Dana's voice trailed off.

In the silence, Francie could hear a door opening down the hall, a shout, a burst of laughter.

"If you want to come home, I think there's still time, but it —"

Francie hadn't heard anything else her mother said. She'd begun packing her suitcase while she was still on the phone.

Two days later, Peter had died. The last thing he'd said was, "You can have my cowboy hat, Francie, my niece."

Francie, shaken, had returned to Smith a week later and hung the hat on her wall.

The days had passed, then weeks, then months. Sadie, too, died, curling up on her bed one evening and not moving when Dana tried to rouse her for breakfast the next morning. Dana had put her house on the market then and moved back to New York, and Francie had grown used to dividing her vacations between Princeton and Manhattan.

Then had come graduation and her search for a job in publishing. September rolled around; she was still unemployed; and she accepted Matthew's offer to continue to live with him and Maura, to babysit occasionally, but to use the rest of her time to try her hand at writing seriously. She sent out one poem and short story after another and began writing a novel. Every day, she checked the mailbox for a letter saying that something she had written had been accepted for publication and would soon appear in print.

Every day, there was nothing. Well, not nothing. There was mail for Matthew and Maura, and letters from Claudia and Sue for Francie. But no envelope bearing the news that Francie would be following in her grandfather Zander's literary footsteps.

Until December 31st. Late that afternoon, Francie had been in her room getting ready for a New Year's Eve party when she heard a small knock on her door, and before she could announce that she was indecent, Jordan had burst inside. Seeing his big sister standing before the mirror in her bra and panties, he'd squeezed his eyes shut, squawked, "Ew!" and handed her an envelope. "You got mail," he'd said, and fled from the room.

Francie looked at the return address. Miller Press, in Pennsylvania. She opened it, read it dully, then read it again and shouted, "Matthew! Maura! I did it! I sold something!"

It was a poem. She had sold it to a very small press, but it was the beginning of her writing career; Francie was sure of it. She had practically skipped to the party and greeted all her old friends — Kaycee, Amy, Beth, Dale, and Isabel, who were back in Princeton for the holidays — with her happy news. They were clustered around her, congratulating her, when she'd felt a hand on her shoulder, turned, and found herself facing George Noble.

"Surprise," he'd said. "Happy new year."

Francie's smile had widened into a grin and she'd thrown her arms around him. They separated from the others and spent the evening together. When the ball had dropped in Times Square, the party guests crowded around Amy's television, counting down the last ten seconds of 1992, and George pulled Francie to him and kissed her lightly on the lips.

Six months later, they'd gotten married. Kaycee was Francie's maid of honor, Claudia and Amy were bridesmaids, Jordan was the ring bearer, and Sarah was the flower girl. Francie and George had moved to an apartment off Route 1, and George had landed his dream job as a teacher at Littlebrook Elementary School. Francie continued writing, and sold a short story to the *New Yorker.*

Now on this warm Friday in July, they found themselves standing in front of Francie's childhood home.

"So?" said George. "What do you think? We can just barely afford it."

Francie stared at the house for several more moments. At last, she said, "Let's do it."

Then she placed her hand over her belly, pulled George to her, smiled gently, and told him about the baby who would be born in February. The baby she would love and protect and shelter from danger.

About the Author

Ann M. Martin is the acclaimed and bestselling author of a number of novels and series, including *Belle Teal*, *A Corner of the Universe* (a Newbery Honor book), *A Dog's Life*, *Here Today*, *P.S. Longer Letter Later* (written with Paula Danziger), the Doll People series (written with Laura Godwin), the Main Street series, and the generation-defining series The Babysitters Club. She lives in New York.